THE ARK OF DUN RUAH

This book is dedicated to my
husband Tony and my son Aidan

Maria Burke

The Ark of Dun Ruah

CURRACH
PRESS

First published in 2012 by
CURRACH PRESS
55A Spruce Avenue,
Stillorgan Industrial Park,
Blackrock,
Co. Dublin

Cover design by Anú Design
Cover illustration: Maria Burke

Origination by Currach Press
Printed by MPG Books Group Ltd

ISBN 978 1 85607 794 1

Acknowledgements

Thanks to everyone who encouraged me to write the book.
To Anna and Sarah Daly, Ivetta Jordanov and family,
Tina and Chris Noon, Helen Murphy, Helen Peffer,
Jo Pottier, Valerie O'Regan and Martin Kelleher.
Thanks also to the staff and families of Currach Press.

N

W   E

S

TWO PEAKS

Waterfall

Abbey of Dun
Ruah

Red Beak's
Palace

The Ark of Dun Ruah

Sea of Sorrows
Queen Kiki's
Crystal Chamber
k Lake
Lake Caves
LONE PEAK
MOUNTAINS
NDS
BARREN LANDS
Pilgrim's Way
Cooley House
CORACLE
Old Chapel
Blow Hole
Cave Village
SEA CAVES
Shipwrecks
Sea of Sorrows
EYRIE
ISLAND

Fact File on Eagles

- Harpy and Philippine eagles have a wingspan of two and a half metres. They use their massive talons to kill and carry off prey as large as deer.

- Eagles have very good eyesight. They see five basic colours. Humans only see three. They can spot a rabbit two miles away.

- Eagles lay a clutch of two eggs. Usually the older chick kills the younger sibling and the adults don't stop it.

- An eagle's territory can range over 100 square miles. To defend territory or attract a mate, eagles put on spectacular displays such as death defying swoops and daring stunts e.g. fighting and locking talons with another bird and then free falling in spirals to the ground.

- They can dive at speeds of up to 100 miles per hour.

- A group of eagles is called a convocation or a kettle.

- An eagle has at least 7,000 feathers.

- Eagles' nests can weigh up to one and a half tonnes. That's the weight of a large car.

- Giant Eagles once lived in New Zealand and had a 10-foot wingspan. They are reputed to have carried off men, women and children to devour.

- Giant Eagles were thought to have become extinct 800 years ago but there were reported sightings of them in the 19th century in remote mountainous areas.

- The Golden Eagle was extinct in Ireland for 100 years. It has been reintroduced to Co. Donegal from Scotland.

- Extinct creatures have been known to reappear. The Caspian Horse was thought to be extinct for centuries and has now been found. So was the Madagascar Serpent Eagle, the Ivory Billed Woodpecker and the Javan Elephant.

Fact File on Owls

- Not all owls hoot. They screech, whistle, bark, click and hiss. Their calls can be heard up to a mile away. Baby owls make snoring sounds when looking for food.

- Owls have no teeth. They swallow their prey whole and twelve hours later cough up the feathers, bones and fur in football-shaped pellets.

- Unable to move their eyes, owls turn their entire heads to see in different directions. They rotate their heads up to 270 degrees.

- Owls have specialised feathers with fringes to muffle sound when they fly.

- The tufts of feathers on top of owls' heads are for display only. Owls' ears are hidden on the facial disc behind the eyes. They can open and close their ears.

- Owls have long, hooked bills. Concealed by feathers, the bills look smaller than they are.

- The owl's flattened, facial disk funnels sound to its ears and magnifies it up to ten times. They hear noises humans can't detect and can hear a mouse 60 feet away.

- An owl has three eyelids: one for blinking, one for sleeping and one for keeping the eye clean and healthy.

- A barn owl can eat up to 1,000 mice each year, and farmers like to attract them.

- Owls have zygodactyl feet with two toes pointing forward and two toes pointing backward. This gives them a stronger grip.

- Most female owls are larger, more aggressive and often more richly coloured than their male counterparts.

- A group of owls is called a parliament, wisdom or study.

- Blue Owls are extremely rare but an Irish teenager called Simon Macken claims to have one living in his loft.

CHAPTER 1

The Blue Owl

The Blue Owl flew through the busy streets with six Giant Eagles in pursuit. The streamlined bodies of the huge eagle predators swept over the startled crowds. Their penetrating eyes scanned the partygoers who were arriving in the town to attend the Fire Fair. Bent on their evil mission, the eagles honed in on their single victim. They flew low, clipping the heads of stunned pedestrians. The crowds scattered, running for cover.

The Blue Owl knew he was almost within their grasp. He felt an icy fear clawing his heart. At lightning speed the eagles gained on him every moment. His only chance was to keep low and try to lose them among the crowds. If he shook them off he'd make for the Swishtree Forest. There the trees would hide him.

He came to a narrow alley between two tall rickety buildings and took a sudden turn into it. Twisting his head sharply, he craned his neck backwards to see if the eagles were following him.

Then, with a screech, he crashed.

Kerry Macken took the force of the blow straight into the forehead. She fell backwards onto an old terrace, hit a metal garage door and collapsed. A shock of crimson hair fell over her wide blue eyes and a bright red bundle flew out of her arms. She sat stunned on the ground trying to focus on the owl as he reeled across the dim alley. He landed fluttering and spluttering in the gutter.

'Pod, you daft owl, you nearly killed me!' cried Kerry. 'And now look. I've dropped the Lord Mayor's new coat. It'll be ruined!'

Scrambling to her feet, she limped across the cobbled street and straightened her leather jacket. She retrieved the red bundle and examined it closely. Satisfied that it was still intact, she turned her attention to the agitated owl.

'Where are you going in such a hurry?' she asked him. He flitted nervously around her shoulders.

'The eagles are after me,' panted Pod. Attaching himself firmly to Kerry's shoulder he dug his beak into her ear. 'They're coming around the corner. This time they'll get me. I'm done for!'

'Not eagles again!' said Kerry, smoothing her hair. She scanned the alley and then hobbled towards the corner, clutching her bundle. Pod burrowed deep inside her jacket while she looked up and down the busy street.

'There are lots of people around, but I can't see any eagles.'

Pods voice trembled. 'They're after me, I tell you.'

'Maybe they were chasing a cat or a rat or something else,' said Kerry. 'Oh Pod, stop shaking! It's not good to be getting so worked up. You'll give yourself another dose of the hiccups. Don't you remember the last time you got upset? You got such a fit of hiccups. It lasted an entire week!'

'Those eagles have been following me around for days,' moaned Pod. 'Everywhere I go I see them watching me and waiting to pounce. And they're so big and evil looking. It's torture living like this. I can't sleep. I can't eat—'

'Oh Pod, what a terrible imagination you have! Last summer you complained that monkeys were following you everywhere. Now it's Giant Eagles. All this excitement is not good for your nerves.'

'But the monkeys really were following me everywhere last summer,' replied Pod. His eyes began to twitch.

'Don't you remember that horrible circus that was camped at the edge of the town? I'll never forget how nasty those little monkeys were—'

'Pod, I feel really sorry for you but I can't talk right now,' said Kerry. 'I've got to get to the town hall to meet the Lord Mayor. The Grand Opening of the Fire Fair is just about to start and he's waiting for his new coat. It's a good job you didn't damage it you silly old owl! It's taken me months to finish.'

'I may be old but I am not silly. This is real! Those eagles are out to get me and I can't for the life of me figure out why. You should see the size of them. They're deadly. You've got to believe me, Kerry – before it's too late for all of us.'

'Pod, I do believe you. But there's no sign of any eagles around here now. So pull yourself together. Go home and calm down. Now I've got to find Simon. Have you seen him anywhere? He promised he'd be home early, to come with me to meet the Lord Mayor. And of course he's gone missing again. Wouldn't you know? It's always the same with that brother of mine. He's never in the right place at the right time.'

'I did see him somewhere,' said Pod, blinking his large amber eyes. 'Where was it? Let me think. Oh yes, I saw him hanging around St John's Square, shuffling around doorways like he was up to something. At least he was there a few minutes ago when the procession started. That was before those eagles saw me and came after me and—'

'Thanks, Pod. You're a big help. I'll go there now. Promise me you'll go straight home for a rest. I'll talk to you later and we'll sort out the problem with the eagles. I'll be back after the Grand Opening is over.'

'Me, go back to Macken Cottage on my own?' exclaimed Pod. 'Are you crazy? Don't you realise that those eagles have it under 24-hour surveillance? I wouldn't stand a chance back there all on my own. I can't bear to think of what they'd do to me if they got their horrible, sharp claws all over me—'

'Pod, I promise I'll be straight home after the Mayor's Grand Opening. You know how important this is. He's waiting right now for this coat I've designed for him. And it's a big break for me. I must go.'

'Go then. But I know who my real friends are. The swishtrees are the only ones who will protect me. Where else can I go to hide from those vicious eagle giants?'

Before Kerry could reply Pod flew up into the air and, with a great flurry of blue feathers, fled in the direction of the Swishtree Forest.

Kerry sighed. Pod's behaviour was very odd lately. He had been talking about Giant Eagles for days and was constantly fidgeting and looking over his shoulder. His huge amber eyes never closed and his mind was obsessed with the threat of eagles. At night he flitted nervously back and forth across the loft of Macken Cottage, banging into rafters and disturbing everyone's sleep.

Kerry hurried on to St John's Square searching for her younger brother on the way. Earlier she had checked the shed and outhouses of Macken Cottage, where Simon was usually busy doing one of his crazy experiments with explosives. But he was nowhere to be found. The trouble with Simon was that he was never there when she wanted him. And he always popped up in places where he was least expected. He was one of those boys who kept getting stuck into things that were none of his business. Kerry tried her best to look after him but his curious interests and hobbies caused a lot of trouble between them.

The candlelight procession wound its way around the ancient streets of Kilbeggin on its way to St John's Square. A long line of monks clad in white, hooded robes chanted verses in deep harmonies as they marched in unison. They moved slowly, carrying long, tapered candles that flickered in the deepening twilight. Kerry skirted along the edges, searching through the crowds as the procession progressed. She followed the monks through the narrow streets and right up to the doors of St John's Cathedral.

Her eyes scanned the sea of faces looking for Simon. Some quick movement above the huge gothic doorway stopped Kerry in her tracks. She studied the ancient stone carvings. A host of menacing gargoyles leered down from the heights, their jaws gaping at the crowds who followed the monks' procession into the cathedral.

She looked closely at one of the gargoyles. Its eyes seemed to be moving. Her heart leaped as two red beams of light flashed through the stone carved eye sockets and flooded down over the crowds. Kerry followed the laser-like beams with her eyes as they fell upon a side door of the cathedral, saturating it with an eerie red glow. There she spotted a tall, hooded figure lurking in the shadows under a pointed archway. The laser beams scanned him as he gazed straight up at their source behind the stone gargoyles.

Suddenly, an enormous bird flew out from behind the carvings and swooped down, plunging its talons into the shoulders of the man. A piercing cry shattered the peaceful procession as the victim burst from the doorway struggling with the attacking bird. The creature's mighty claws sank deeper into the man's cloak; its eyes flashed red as it pecked savagely at the man's hood. But to Kerry's astonishment the man counterattacked with a stunning blow to the bird's head. A blinding flash of light engulfed the bird as the man raised his right arm. The bird rallied and as fast as it had descended it flew back up to the gargoyles once again, vanishing behind them.

Pulling his long, grey cloak closely around him, the man retreated into the shadows. His face was entirely concealed under a deep hood. Then he vanished into the church.

A sharp voice in her right ear caused Kerry to jump.

'Did you see that Giant Eagle?'

'Simon. You scared the life out of me,' said Kerry. 'Where have you been? I've been looking for you everywhere.'

Simon, her younger brother, was still gazing up at the gargoyles, his eyes transfixed, his cheeks on fire and his mop of rusty brown hair standing on end.

'A Giant Eagle,' continued Simon. 'Boy, what a beauty! Did you see his claws, Kerry? Sharp as steel! But what's a rare bird like that doing in this boring old town? That's what I'd like to know. Those creatures are strong enough to carry a fully grown man. I thought they were extinct. Did you see it, Kerry? Wasn't it powerful! But hey, where did the man go? I'm going after him into the church.'

'Simon! Don't you remember one single thing? You promised to come with me to the town hall to meet the Lord Mayor. I've been trying to find you.'

'What? Oh I know, I know. Just hang on a second, I've got to talk to that man and find out why the eagle attacked him. I'll be back in a minute, really I will.'

'But it's none of your business and I …'

Simon was already running through the archway and before Kerry knew it he had disappeared into the cathedral after the man with the grey cloak.

CHAPTER 2

An Invitation

Kerry paced the marble tiles under the Gothic doorway of St John's Cathedral. Simon still hadn't returned and the Lord Mayor was waiting in the town hall for his designer coat. Kerry dreaded the thought of going there alone. She had worked long and hard on this coat, specially designed for the Grand Opening of the World Fire Fair. It was an opportunity to showcase her work to the town and the world beyond. While Kerry shied away from the spotlight, Simon loved it. Only a month ago he had brazenly walked up to the Lord Mayor at the town's Young Designer Exhibition. He showed him Kerry's work and talked him into giving her a commission to design him a new coat.

It was at times like this that Kerry missed her mother. She knew that if she had been alive she would have been proud of her daughter tonight. It was only a year since she died and Kerry had been forced to drop out of school and start her own business to make a living. She loved designing clothes but it was always a struggle to make ends meet.

A fluttering in the great arches above startled her. She looked up at the vaults, hoping that the Giant Eagle hadn't returned. Then she saw two sets of wings fluttering to and fro. A couple of little, dark green birds descended onto the steps beside her, their bright eyes flashing. The larger one fluffed out his creamy breast and the little one perched softly on Kerry's shoulder. She was relieved to see that it was her swiftail friends Timmy and Dot who lived with Pod in the loft of Macken Cottage.

'We've been looking for you everywhere,' said Dot. 'Are you OK? Why aren't you at the town hall? It's almost time for the Grand Opening.'

'I'm waiting for Simon to come back. He was here a moment ago and then he went running off into the cathedral after a man who was attacked by a Giant Eagle. He promised to go with me to the town hall. But now I think it's gone clean out of his head.'

'Let me come with you,' said Dot. 'I'd love to meet the Mayor.'

'And I'll go look for Simon,' said Timmy. 'If he's in the cathedral I'll find him and make sure that he follows you down to the town hall.'

'Oh Timmy, that would be great! And I'd love if you came with me, Dot. I'd better not keep the Lord Mayor of Kilbeggin waiting any longer.'

'Well, off with you,' said Timmy. 'The Mayor needs that

beautiful coat of yours to perform the Grand Opening. He'll be delighted when he sees it. But you'd better hurry up. If you don't get there soon he might wear something else.'

Timmy flew into the church. And with a fresh burst of courage Kerry followed Dot through the narrow streets and down to the town hall.

The arrival of the World Fire Fair to Kilbeggin had created quite a stir. It was the first time an event of this size had ever come to town and a packed festival of dazzling spectacles was promised. Outside the town hall a great bonfire blazed. Barbecues burned and all the mouth-watering aromas of outdoor cooking filled the air. Trees glittered with flickering lanterns and the central fountain blazed with light. Showers of red, orange and yellow cascaded as people gathered for the Grand Opening. Everyone was waiting for the Lord Mayor to open the festival with the launch of a glittering fireworks display.

Kerry and Dot found the Mayor's private entrance at the side of the town hall. Dot pulled the bell chord and a butler dressed in gold livery opened the door. He informed Kerry that the Mayor was expecting her. She followed him to the Mayor's private chambers with Dot firmly perched on her shoulder. The butler ushered them into a huge, ornate sitting room.

'Miss Kerry Macken and her friend … ahem … Dot,' he announced.

The Mayor was sitting on a red sofa at the top of the chamber with a tall, silver-haired lady at his side. He jumped to his feet as soon as he saw Kerry and bounded across the room to greet her.

'At last you're here. Well done, my girl. I thought you'd never make those final adjustments. Especially when I put on that bit of extra weight last week! Show me my lovely new coat and let me try it on. But where are my manners? My dear Kerry, I want to introduce you to my very special guest. I've been telling her all about your work. President Lumina, this is my talented designer Kerry Macken.'

The tall, silver-haired lady rose with great dignity from the sofa. She was wearing a stunning full-length, gold-sequined dress.

'I'm delighted to introduce you to one another,' said the Lord Mayor. 'Lady Lumina is the President of the Land of Fire. She is waiting to get the first glimpse of my new coat.'

'It's great to meet you, Kerry,' said President Lumina. 'I've been hearing all about the coat you've made for Frederick. And I know you based it on the theme of fire. It sounds divine. Try it on, Frederick and let's have a look at it.'

Kerry took the bright red coat from its wrapping and helped the Mayor into it. With great fuss, the butler was ordered to wheel in a full-length mirror. Kerry did up the buttons and straightened the shoulders and collar. Then they all peered into the mirror.

'Wow! It's beautiful, Kerry, absolutely top class,' proclaimed President Lumina.

'It makes me look younger,' cried the Mayor.

'Yes and thinner,' President Lumina added while the Mayor blushed.

'I love the fiery reds you've used and, look, this gold stitching shimmers like real flames. It's so detailed. Quite exquisite! This is certainly an extraordinary talent you have, dear child. I simply must get you to make one for me too. Sometimes I have four or five functions to attend in a day and I'm always looking for talented designers to come up with a new image for me. Why don't you visit me in the Land of Fire? You could design an entire new wardrobe for me. I would pay you handsomely, of course, and give you a very good time. What do you say?'

'Well, thank you, Lady Lumina. I'm very honoured. But do you mind if I think about it?' Kerry asked.

'What's there to think about? I know you'd love it! If Frederick can spare you for a few months you can leave for my home in Fire City next week. There's nothing to worry about. All your expenses will be covered.'

'I'd love to go, but the problem is that I have a younger brother. He's just a schoolboy and I can't leave him here on his own.'

'Then bring him with you,' insisted President Lumina.

❁❁❁

Simon was fighting his way through the crowds that had filtered into St John's Cathedral. He was still searching for the man with the hooded cloak. The monks were chanting and it was difficult to see anything in the flickering candlelight. He was just about to go back outside to rejoin Kerry when he spotted the man in the grey cloak ahead of him. People were filing into the pews but the grey-cloaked man was making for a side aisle. As the crowd suddenly parted, Simon found a way through and darted after him. The man took a right turn into a side altar and skirted the railings behind it. Simon followed. He was curious to know why an almost extinct bird would attack a man in such a savage way. He also wondered what kind of power the man possessed that was strong enough to overpower a Giant Eagle.

The man in the grey cloak stopped abruptly. It was as if he knew what Simon was thinking. He turned to face him and suddenly reared up to a great height. He stared down into Simon's eyes. A deep hood still shaded his face. But Simon sensed that the man was warning him to keep his distance. Penetrating green eyes flashed from under the dark cowl and bored into Simon, almost piercing through his skull. A wave of fear coursed through his veins causing his head to spin. He staggered into a pew and righted himself in time to see the man vanishing behind the side altar. Simon rushed after him and jumped over the altar railings. He scanned the area. There were no doors or windows visible, only stone walls towering up on each side. The man had vanished.

Then light breeze brushed his face. Something landed on his shoulder.

'What are you doing hiding behind here?' asked Timmy. 'I've been looking for you everywhere.'

'You nearly gave me a heart attack,' said Simon. 'Did you see the way that man disappeared? He was standing here right before my eyes one moment and the next he was gone. I can't find any trace of him.'

'You've got to come with me to the town hall right now,'

pleaded Timmy. 'No more chasing after disappearing men. Kerry is relying on you. This meeting is important to her, to both of you.'

Casting a final look around the altar in the hope of catching one more glimpse of the man with the green eyes, Simon tore himself away from his quest. He followed Timmy out of the church. St John's Square was still deserted but Simon felt he was being followed by hidden eyes. He paused to take a final look at the gargoyles on the cathedral walls.

'Timmy, can you see something red flashing behind those carvings?'

'It's probably just reflections from the Fire Fair.'

'No. There's something still up there,' said Simon. 'I think I can see eagles with red eyes. I have to find out what they're doing here.'

'There's no time for this Simon,' said Timmy. 'Come on. Kerry really needs your support right now. I promised her I'd bring you straight to the town hall.'

Simon reluctantly gave in and followed Timmy to St John's Square. The streets were filling up with merrymakers. Bonfires blazed in the distant hills. Flickering lanterns illuminated doorways and alleys. Along the streets flamethrowers and fire jugglers were displaying their skills.

A man on stilts suddenly leaned towards Simon. He was eating bright red flames and breathing out smoke that swirled eerily up into the night sky. A juggler tossed fireballs high into the air and spun them into kaleidoscopes of colour and light. Flamethrowers swirled batons of fire over their heads, then wove them between their arms and legs.

Just as Simon and Timmy reached the door of the town hall an enormous eagle engulfed in fire and smoke flew across the sky above them. It was followed by a menacing army of evil- looking birds. They swooped towards the crowds causing screams of surprise and horror. People scattered across the square, fleeing for cover.

'Simon, come on inside,' called Timmy.

Simon was relieved to see the butler standing at the open doorway, waiting to escort them to the Mayor's quarters. His hair was tussled and his face was flushed with excitement as the butler showed them into the chamber.

'Master Simon Macken and his friend … ahem … Timmy,' said the butler.

'Hello, Simon,' said the Mayor. 'It's great to see you again.'

'Simon, we've been waiting for you,' said President Lumina. 'What a handsome boy you are with your rusty head of hair. I was talking to your sister about a very interesting proposal. How would you like to travel to the Land of Fire on a business trip with her?'

'What?' Simon's face lit up. 'The Land of Fire, I've always dreamt of going to the Land of Fire. Is this true, Kerry?'

'I haven't decided yet,' said Kerry. 'There's your school to think about!'

'Don't worry about school,' exclaimed President Lumina. 'Simon can study with my own children. And we have the best teachers. We'll take good care of him.'

Kerry looked at her younger brother's excited face.

'But Simon would miss his experiments. He's got some unusual stuff that he works at in our shed … it's not exactly the normal sort of thing that boys do …'

'He seems like a normal boy to me,' said the Mayor. 'What could be so unusual about his activities?'

'I'm an inventor,' said Simon with a grin.

'But that involves experimenting with home-made explosives in the garden shed,' said Kerry. 'He's set it on fire several times and I know it wouldn't be safe—'

'But this is perfect,' cried President Lumina. 'We love inventors. We can teach him all about explosives and pyrotechnics in the Land of Fire. He'll be right at home with us. We are at the cutting edge of fire technology.'

'But it can be dangerous,' said Kerry. 'I'm always so worried that he'll set himself on fire or blow our whole house up. He might destroy your home too and ruin the whole trip!'

'Stop exaggerating Kerry!' interrupted Simon.

'Now, now my dear, don't you worry about Simon. The Land of Fire is the safest place you could take a boy with such interests. At least with us he can learn to make explosions in a safe and controlled environment without creating any accidents. Why, he might even make a career out of it.'

'Kerry, don't you see', said Simon, 'this is the perfect opportunity for both of us. Open your eyes. If you want us to stay together and keep our home we've got to grab this chance. You said yourself we haven't got enough to live on.'

'I think we'd better settle this matter now,' said the Mayor. 'It's time for me to open the World Fire Fair and I'm late already. The crowds are waiting.'

'What do you say, Kerry?' asked President Lumina.

'Well, if you don't mind Simon coming along …?'

'I'll be delighted to have Simon! Don't give it another thought. Oh and Frederick, will you please make sure that my two new friends and their dear little birds are on board the ship bound for the Land of Fire on Monday night? It leaves from Corkscrew Harbour at midnight.'

'Certainly, my dear,' said the Mayor. 'I'll do everything in my power to get them there. They'll have a wonderful voyage on board the legendary ship, the Ark of Dun Ruah.'

CHAPTER 3

Fireworks and Explosives

On the outskirts of Kilbeggin, in the foothills of the Purple Mountains, Macken Cottage nestled. The Swishtree Forest skirted the cottage garden and wrapped itself like a giant green scarf all the way around the town of Kilbeggin.

Every now and again a loud bang rattled the garden shed where Simon was working on his latest invention. He was in a hurry to get it finished before they set out for the Land of Fire. Timmy and Dot flew back and forth, helping Kerry to sort and pack their things for the journey. Another loud explosion from the shed sent Kerry running to the back door.'

'Simon,' she called. 'What are you doing out there? Please don't make me call the fire brigade again.'

'Everything's under control,' Simon's voice replied from the depths of the shed. 'And I'm nearly finished. This is my best invention yet. Wait 'til you see my 'Handy Matches,' Kerry. I think I've got the formula right at last.'

Kerry shook her head. 'I hope they cure him of his obsession with lighting matches in the Land of Fire. He can't get much worse.'

'Speaking of obsessions, has anybody seen Pod?' asked Timmy.

'Hiding in the forest, no doubt,' said Dot.

'But we still haven't told him about our trip to the Land of Fire,' said Timmy, 'and we can't leave him behind.'

'He was right about those eagles though,' said Kerry. 'Everyone in Kilbeggin is talking about them. They've been raiding people's gardens and sheds and causing so much trouble.'

'Trouble,' hooted a deep voice from the window.

There, perched high on a ledge, stood Pod with his thick crop of blue feathers gleaming in the moonlight and his amber eyes flashing.

'I told you they were trouble. But you didn't believe me. This Fire Fair is the worst thing that's ever happened to Kilbeggin. All sorts of peculiar folk coming in here, poking their noses in our business! If it wasn't for the Fire Fair those eagles would never have come here in the first place.'

'Oh, Pod, we're glad you're home,' said Timmy. 'Have you heard the news? We're all going to the Land of Fire.'

'The Land of Fire!' screeched Pod. 'Is this some kind of a joke?'

'Kerry has been invited there by President Lumina,' said Dot, 'to be her personal fashion designer.'

'You're out of your minds,' said Pod. 'What business have you going on a dangerous journey like that?'

'It's a great opportunity for Kerry to get her business started.'

'But now is a terrible time to travel,' said Pod. 'There are dark and evil forces at work out there in the world. The swishtrees are moaning. I haven't heard them moan like that since I was a boy. The signs are clear. Wicked things are stirring. Things I wouldn't dare speak of.'

'But it's all arranged, and we were hoping you'd come with us,' said Kerry.

Pod's eyes began to twitch. 'Then cancel it! This is not the time for foolish and risky adventures. You have no idea of the evil that is lurking out there.'

'But we're going on a ship,' said Timmy. 'You've always said that ships are the safest way to travel.'

'Not in these troubled times,' warned Pod. 'Nothing and nobody is safe. And a ship is no place for an elderly owl like me. Ships are full of hungry rats and cats all vying to get their teeth into a tasty bird. No this is a terrible idea. Stop all this nonsense and stay at home in Kilbeggin.'

'Our passage is booked,' said Kerry. 'President Lumina of the Land of Fire paid for everything. She has invited me there to design a new wardrobe for her. I have to earn a living, Pod. Simon needs to be fed and sent to school and I've had a lot of bills since Mom died last year. I'm barely able to make ends meet as it is. Without this trip we can't afford to keep our home here in Macken Cottage. And I don't want to sell it. It's the only thing we have left!'

'Go without me then,' said Pod. 'All of you. I'll stay here

where I belong.'

'Please come with us, Pod,' pleaded Kerry. 'The Land of Fire is a beautiful place. It's a land of opportunity.'

'Opportunity,' Pod snorted.

'But we badly need a wise old head like yours to help us on our journey,' pleaded Kerry. 'We'd be lost without you, Pod, you know that.'

'And what if those eagles keep tormenting you here?' added Dot. 'You'll be stuck inside all alone every day, terrified out of your wits.'

Pod let out a huge hiccup and before he had a chance to recover himself Simon burst through the back door.

'I've done it,' he cried. 'My matches are ready. In fact they're perfect. And now for the demonstration you've all been waiting for—'

'No Simon!' cried Kerry. 'The last time you did a demonstration in the house, you nearly took the roof off. It took us a whole week to clean up the mess.'

'Don't worry,' said Simon digging into the rubbish bin and pulling out fistfuls of old food scraps and wrappers. He quickly packed them into the fire grate and took a large box of matches from his pocket. Flicking it open, he picked out a long, bright green match and struck it.

A mighty crack rocked the floorboards and a dazzling plume of green smoke burst from the match. Sending blinding flashes darting across the room, it swirled into the fireplace and hovered over the rubbish. A rapid series of sparks and flames shot out of the fireplace causing Pod to flee with a shriek into the rafters. A quick succession of bangs and snaps followed and an exploding stream of flashing emerald fireworks cascaded into the room.

'Simon, I said no fireworks in the house,' screamed Kerry.

'Sorry. I couldn't resist it,' said Simon, calling their attention back to the fire.

'Now here's the important bit. Watch this!'

The kitchen rubbish popped and hissed. It then started to swirl in the grate. Plastic bottles shrivelled, newspapers fizzled and lumps of food shrunk into small nuggets that looked like dark green coal. Then a circle of yellow flames sprang from the coals and flared up into a glittering blaze. But, to Kerry's relief, within a few moments the whole thing quietly settled down into a warm, steady and well-behaved fire.

'That fire will last for hours,' said Simon, clapping his hands. 'And it runs on every kind of rubbish. No need to buy any more wood or coal. It costs nothing and burns up all the old waste in the house.'

'This must be magic or trickery!' proclaimed Pod from the rafters. 'Open the window or we'll all be poisoned to death.'

'Don't worry,' said Simon, 'it's science! I've been experiment-ing with gases for months and this one is perfectly safe. It's a harmless eco-friendly gas that accelerates waste decomposition and transforms old rubbish into solid fuel. The result is a great long-lasting fire. It's simple and cheap.'

'It is a nice fire,' said Dot, 'but what about the other matches in the box here? They're all different colours.'

'See this white one,' said Simon, pulling a tall, thin match with a long stem from the box. He struck the match and raised it over their heads. The match produced a white flame that crystallised into a solid beam of light that shone like a laser, projecting a powerful ray onto the rafters above them. 'This one lasts for a few hours. It's very handy if you can't find a torch.'

'It might be useful in a power cut,' said Kerry. 'You know, Simon, people might be interested in your inventions if you only got rid of the nasty fireworks that go with them. What sane person would allow a box of exploding matches into their house?'

'You'd be surprised,' said Dot. 'That fuel-saving idea is a good one,'

'They'll love it over in the Land of Fire,' said Timmy. 'I think you'll be famous. But show us what the other matches do Simon. What about these orange and blue ones.'

Timmy had perched himself precariously on the edge of the matchbox and was gazing closely in at the contents.

'Hey, be careful Timmy,' said Simon, waving him away. 'Some of them are dangerous. They do all sorts of useful things. But they're not ready. I need to do more work on them. There's not much time left before we leave for the Land of Fire. And I want to bring my best inventions with me.'

Simon snatched up his box of matches and exited through the back door.

'Don't wait up for me,' he called.

'I worry about that boy,' said Pod, now perched on Kerry's shoulder, his head tilting to one side. 'If it wasn't for me that shed would be burned down long ago. I don't know how many times I've found it on fire and raised the alarm. If I wasn't around to watch over him we'd all be dead ...'

'Then come with us,' challenged Kerry. 'If you want to keep him alive, come with us to the Land of Fire.'

CHAPTER 4

The Ark of Dun Ruah

Corkscrew Harbour was situated in a narrow, winding creek. It was close to midnight when Kerry, Simon, Pod and the swiftails followed the coastal path from Kilbeggin to the harbour. Kerry marvelled at the endless twists and turns the brightly lit estuary took on its way to the sea. A large ship was docked at the quayside with the name 'Ark of Dun Ruah' painted on its side. A queue of passengers waited to board. Kerry looked around at her travelling companions.

Three very small men were conversing loudly at the quayside. They had red faces with long noses and very large ears. They were dressed in faded lumber shirts and trousers that barely reached down to the top of their boots. The discussion was growing louder and Kerry could see angry fists raised in the air. One of them made several rude exclamations and snorts. The others shook their fists at him and stamped their feet.

'What an odd-looking bunch,' whispered Kerry.

'They're the Frumpets,' said Pod. 'They're tribal folk from the Swishtree Forest. They mainly live on wild mushrooms and berries and I sometimes see them in Kilbeggin scrounging around looking for food.'

'I wish they'd stop fighting,' said Kerry.

'Oh they never stop fighting,' said Pod. 'They fight every day. Except, of course, at the weekends when they spend all day in bed.'

A tall, hooded man in a dark cloak arrived and slipped into the line of people behind them. Kerry looked at him closely. She wondered if it was the same man who had been attacked by the eagle at the cathedral door. It was difficult to see his face under the deep, grey hood. His movements made him seem almost like a shadow. She wondered what kind of power he held over the eagle that attacked him that night on St John's Square.

But it was difficult to see in the deepening darkness. The passengers ahead of them had started to board and the queue was moving. Kerry was so tired that it was a struggle trying to keep her eyes open.

Simon tugged her arm. 'Come on. Let's board.'

They moved towards the huge hulking shadow of the tall passenger ship that loomed above them. A man dressed in a monk's habit took Kerry's ticket and helped her on board.

'Enjoy your voyage,' he said. 'Tomorrow we'll be sailing across the Sea of Sorrows.'

'Sea of Sorrows,' said Kerry. 'I hope it's not anything like its name.'

'They say it's bewitched,' said the ticket man, assisting her onto the deck. 'So keep your wits about you.'

'Keep my wits about me. What do you mean?' Kerry asked.

But the ticket man had already turned his back on her. He was attending to the next passenger. A sudden sea breeze blew up and Kerry pulled up the collar of her jacket. She looked around and saw Simon and the birds ahead of her. They had crossed the gangway onto the ship. Again she caught a glimpse of the man with the grey, hooded robe. Somehow he had overtaken them and was moving quickly to the top of the crowd.

'Hey! Isn't that the man who was attacked by the eagle with the red eyes?' exclaimed Simon. 'And look up. What's that on the mast?'

Two red beams of light were scanning the length of the deck. Up on the mast, the dark silhouette of a huge bird was peering down at the passengers with intense red eyes. Kerry shivered.

'I'm going to check it out,' said Simon.

'No. Let's get inside Simon,' pleaded Kerry. 'That eagle is up to no good. And I don't want you getting mixed up in trouble at this hour of the night.'

'Well, I suppose it could wait till the morning,' said Simon, reluctantly eyeing the bird on the mast.

'Of course it can wait,' said Kerry. 'And you promised you wouldn't run off on another wild goose chase.'

Simon acquiesced and they followed the passengers into a

small atrium. From here they climbed a staircase to the top deck where they entered a large cabin. There they said good-night to Pod and the swiftails who took off in search of their own nesting places on board the ship. Inside the cabin there was a long, carpeted lounge. All around the floor, comfortable mattresses were scattered with cosy quilts and cushions thrown over them.

'Just grab one,' said Simon.

And Kerry did. She was so warm and snug under her quilt that the sound of the sea breeze and the lapping of the waves soothed away the memory of the giant bird with the red eyes.

❂❂❂

Kerry awoke to the sound of voices coming from the sea. It was still dark and she couldn't see Simon. His mattress was empty. The voices outside called, 'Kerry … Kerry.' She crept out of her bed and followed them onto the deck.

A large swell rose in the sea and the ship began to toss. She thought she heard Simon's voice calling her from the water. Leaning over the ship's side and clinging to the railings she searched the dark blue seas with her eyes. The ship dipped sharply and caused her to lose her grip. As she tumbled, down towards the water a flock of Giant Eagles appeared above her. The largest eagle seized her with his long razor-like talons.

'Come with me,' he cawed.

Kerry tried to struggle but the eagle carried her over the waves far out over the Sea of Sorrows and onto a rocky island. He dragged her into a dark cave and there sitting on a huge throne sat an Eagle King wearing a golden crown. His red laser-like eyes bored into her head causing her face to burn. A loud ringing pierced her ears. She screamed with pain.

'Ding, ding, ding, ding, ding ...' Kerry suddenly woke from her dream. Sunlight was streaming over her face from an overhead porthole. There was the sound of a bell ringing in the distance.

'Breakfast is ready. Come and get it before it's too late,' chanted a voice from below.

Kerry sat up and saw Simon standing before her.

'Come on,' he said. 'I've just been down to the breakfast cabin to check it out. Those Frumpets are trying to gobble up all the food on this ship. I've never seen such a pack of greedy men in all my life. Are you OK Kerry? You look kind of green.'

Kerry rubbed her eyes and crawled out from under her quilt.

'I've just had a horrible nightmare, Simon. I thought I'd lost you.'

'It was only a dream,' said Simon. 'Come on. I'm hungry.'

Kerry followed him across the lounge, through the exit and down a flight of metal stairs to the atrium. Here they saw the entrance to a large dining cabin. Beside the dining cabin there was a door leading out to the open air deck. They went out to the deck, hoping see the birds. Pod swooped and landed on the ships railing. Then he spotted Simon and flew onto his shoulder. He didn't look happy.

'The nesting accommodation on board this ship is a disgrace,' he said. 'It's draughty and noisy. All those moaning voices coming from the sea kept me awake all night. Now I'll have to find a more comfortable hole before nightfall.'

'I heard voices too,' commented Kerry, 'but I thought it was in a dream.'

'Cheer up you two,' said Simon. 'It's a beautiful day. Look, there's the swiftails. At least they seem to be having a good time.'

Timmy and Dot were circling the deck, soaring, swooping and diving for fish.

'Let's go in and get our breakfast,' said Simon.

Inside the dining cabin a breakfast counter was laid out. The three Frumpets sat with their plates piled high with bacon, sausages, eggs, jam doughnuts and heaps of other goodies. They were stuffing it into their large red mouths at a tremendous rate. Two cooks were serving the food behind the counter. They wore white aprons over brown robes that looked very like monks' habits. The older and fatter-looking cook shook his head when Simon and Kerry approached the counter.

'Not much left here,' he said. 'We can't serve up the food fast enough for those Frumpets. Hurry up. If you don't move fast everything will be gone.'

'Are we the last to arrive?' asked Kerry.

'Yes. And we don't serve owls in here.'

'I beg your pardon,' said Pod, digging his claws into Simon's shoulders.

'Pod, get off my shoulder, you daft old owl,' said Simon. 'Go and get your own breakfast.' He pointed at a porthole. 'Look, Timmy and Dot are out there catching fish. Go after them and get some of your own.'

Timmy and Dot were following the ship, playfully swooping into the choppy sea and then soaring off into the clear blue sky.

'I'm too old to go out there catching fish. I'll have to stay and find myself a rat for my breakfast,' said Pod with a grumble. 'There must be one around here somewhere.' He flew off muttering to himself.

After her breakfast, Kerry sat back and looked around the dining cabin studying her fellow passengers. One of the Frumpets had started to eat the remaining leftovers on the food counter. Another was going around from table to table collecting bacon rinds and scraps. The third was licking his plate.

Kerry thought she saw the hooded man in the darkest corner of the dining cabin. He was so deep in the shadows that she could barely see him. Still wearing the grey cloak with the hood shading his face, she watched him stand up and leave his table.

'Hey, there's that man,' said Simon. 'I'm going to find out what's the story with him and the Giant Eagle.'

Just as Simon rose to leave the table one of the Frumpets ran headlong into him. The Frumpet toppled over on to the floor and rolled around howling and screeching with rage. Simon tried to help the little man to his feet.

'You'd better look where you're going, boy!' said the Frumpet crossly, pushing Simon away. 'If you're not careful my brothers and I will give you a good thrashing.'

'Hey, steady up a bit!' said Simon. 'It wasn't my fault. It was you who crashed into me.'

'Don't you get smart with me, boy!' challenged the Frumpet, raising his fists in the air. 'I'll give you a piece of my—'

'Take it easy,' said Simon, removing a slice of toast from Kerry's plate and waving it in the Frumpet's face. 'Hungry, are we?'

'I'll let you off this time,' said the Frumpet, grabbing the toast. 'That's if you let me lick your plate.'

'What?' Simon cried.

But the Frumpet stood his ground, blocking Simon's path.

'Alright, go on then you can lick my plate. Just move out of my way you little savage.'

'I'm not a savage!' said the Frumpet. 'You watch your mouth.'

But Simon was already past him and scanning the dining area for the hooded man. He spotted him at the far side of the room exiting through the cabin door. This time Simon was determined to catch him.

CHAPTER 5

Cooks and Frumpets

Kerry sat in the dining cabin finishing her last piece of toast and waiting for Simon. She tried to keep her eyes off the Frumpets, who were busy licking every plate in the cabin. Then they started pestering the cooks, raiding the food counter and begging for leftover scraps. Whenever the cooks threw something into the rubbish chute the Frumpets shouted rudely and shook their fists.

At last Simon returned from his search for the man in the grey cloak. He didn't look happy. Slumping down on the seat beside Kerry he scratched his head.

'I've lost him again. I can't figure out where he keeps disappearing to. I've checked everywhere, even the toilets.'

'Hey you,' interrupted a Frumpet, who was staring at Kerry's toast. 'Can I have it?'

'Get stuffed!' replied Simon.

'Don't be so rude Simon,' said Kerry. 'He's just hungry.'

'He couldn't still be hungry after all that food. It's ridiculous how much they eat! Come on, Kerry – finish up. Let's get away from these greedy pests.'

'Be careful what you say, boy,' said the Frumpet. 'More of that and I'll thrash you.'

'Go on then,' said Simon standing up to his full height.

Just then a huge commotion broke out behind them. They looked back to see the two cooks wrestling with the other two Frumpets and trying to beat them out of their way. The Frumpets struggled to get a large bag of leftovers out of the rubbish chute. The third Frumpet abandoned Simon and dashed over to join in the fight. After a tussle, the cooks managed to rescue the bag. Then suddenly they all heard a whirring noise. A set of tall, double doors slid open behind the counter. And the cooks rushed through.

'After them,' cried the Frumpets.

The cooks fended off their attackers and the double doors slid shut, blocking the Frumpets' way through. The whirring noise resumed and faded as it descended into the bowels of the ship.

'They're gone,' shouted the Frumpets. 'They're gone. They've stolen our food. We want our money back.'

The Frumpets clawed at the sliding doors trying to follow the cooks. They combed the walls with their thick little fingers, looking for some way to get through the door. But they failed to get in.

'Now, isn't that interesting,' said Simon. 'The cooks have a private elevator all to themselves so that they can escape from annoying passengers. Good for them. So the kitchen and all the food stores must be located down in one of the lower decks.'

'Let's get out of here Simon,' said Kerry, trying to get him away from the Frumpets. 'I'd like to get some fresh air and to have a look around this ship.'

'Good idea. Let's explore the Ark of Dun Ruah,' replied Simon.

Simon and Kerry left the dining cabin and explored the two top decks of the ship. Opposite the dining cabin was an entrance to a games room and beside that was a small shop run by a man in a brown habit. They explored them both and then went back to the atrium and through the door to the outside deck. But they couldn't find a stairs leading to the lower regions of the ship.

They returned to the inner atrium again and took the main staircase to the top deck. This led to the lounge where they had been sleeping. It had been converted to a dormitory during the night. Now the mattresses had been removed and people were sitting around on comfortable chairs and couches. At the end of the lounge they went through a set of glass doors leading out to an open air sun deck at the rear of the ship. Working their way around to the front of the ship, they found a small flight of steps leading to the navigation room. But it was closed off to passengers.

After exhausting their search of the top deck and finding no stairs down to the lower decks, they went back to the sun deck. Here they sat on some comfortable deckchairs with the rest of the passengers, relaxing, in the mid-morning sunshine.

It wasn't long before Timmy and Dot came to find them.

'Have you seen Pod?' asked Timmy.

'He left us before breakfast to go off to catch a rat,' said Kerry. 'He should be back by now.'

'There's no sign of him anywhere,' said Dot, 'and he told us he would meet us here straight after breakfast. I hope the rat he was looking for didn't get the better of him.'

'I doubt there are any rats on board,' said Kerry. 'This ship looks very clean. We've been having a look around here, trying to find a stairs to the lower decks so we can explore the whole ship. But we can't find any.'

'There are no stairs,' said Timmy. 'It's very unusual. We've been scouting around the lower decks looking for Pod since breakfast. All the portholes have dark glass over them so we can't see through. And it's impossible to find any of the crew because the lower decks are totally separated from the passenger decks up here.'

'But some of the portholes were open', said Dot, 'and I thought I saw monks inside. They were all wearing brown robes with hoods.'

'That's interesting,' said Simon. 'There are a lot of monk-like characters hanging around here. The two cooks were wearing brown habits and so was the ticket man. Did you guys by any chance see a tall fellow in a grey, hooded cloak anywhere?'

'No. We just saw lots of men in brown robes,' said Dot.

'There's got to be a logical explanation for all this,' said Simon, scratching his rusty head of hair. 'If only I could figure it out. From what we've seen so far, this ship is run entirely by monks. They come up to the dining cabin at meal times and then they leave in their private elevator. The passengers have no access to the lower decks. And the monks are living down there hidden behind tinted portholes. It's all a bit of a mystery.'

'I wonder why the passengers aren't allowed into the lower parts of the ship,' said Kerry. 'Maybe the monk's belong to an enclosed order. Or they could be criminals dressed up as monks and hiding a terrible secret. Those voices I heard in my dream last night were so real.'

'Well, your imagination is pretty lively today!' said Simon. 'But let's not jump to conclusions until we find Pod.'

'Kerry isn't the only one hearing voices,' said Timmy. 'Right now we are crossing the Sea of Sorrows. The seabirds we met on the ocean this morning told us all about the troubled waters. They said that the waters are enchanted and that many ships have disappeared around here. And we've been hearing voices coming from the sea too.'

'All right then – here are the facts,' said Simon. 'The sea is enchanted. Last night there was an almost extinct Giant Eagle on board scanning the upper decks. Poor old Pod is missing. And there's a suspicious man in a grey, hooded cloak prowling around, who manages to disappear each time I try to catch up with him.'

'So what's the connection?' asked Kerry.

'Well, we saw how the Giant Eagle attacked the man with the grey cloak in Kilbeggin. And pretty savage it was too! We know that Pod was tormented by the same eagles. Now one of them is on this ship and he may still be after Pod. He might even have got to him already and hurt him. We've got to do a proper search for Pod. Let's go back up and check the two top decks properly. Timmy and Dot, you search the rest of the ship and the seas around it. And keep an eye out for eagles. We'll meet back here in an hour.'

The little group of friends all went their separate ways, searching for Pod and asking everyone they met if they had seen him. An hour later they were all back on the top deck. And no one had any news.

'This isn't like Pod not to turn up,' said Kerry. 'He always arrives exactly when he says he will. Something must have happened to him.'

'Maybe we're overreacting,' said Timmy. 'It's possible that he just nodded off to sleep somewhere.'

'Pod doesn't nod off to sleep,' said Dot. 'He is very fussy about where he nests and he always sleeps with one eye open. No, I think something's wrong. He's been gone for hours. Maybe he flew in through one of those tinted portholes on the lower decks and got into trouble.'

'Well, I can hear the lunch bell', said Simon, 'and that means the dining room is open. I'm going to have a chat with the two cooks and see what's going on around here. They might know something about what happened to Pod.'

'We'll keep an eye out while you're gone,' called Timmy.

When Kerry and Simon arrived at the dining cabin the three Frumpets were already fighting to get first place in the queue for lunch. They were stirring up a noisy racket. The cook's voice could be heard over their cries.

'I'm going to ban you three from the dining cabin if you don't behave yourselves right now and that means you will get absolutely nothing to eat for the entire voyage. Now get yourselves back down to the end of the line. You can wait until everyone else has been fed.'

Looks of disappointment began to register on the Frumpets' faces. Their mouths were open, ready to protest when the cook picked two of them up by the ears and shook them violently.

'Do what you are told, or no food,' he said, dropping them at the end of the line.

Kerry and Simon sat at a little table near a porthole and tried to eat some lunch. Simon waited for the cooks to finish serving and for a chance to talk to them alone. Kerry looked out at the deep blue sea. She could see an island off in the distance. It looked very mountainous and rugged. Scores of birds circled above it in the distant grey skies.

Finally the serving finished and Simon approached the head cook.

'Have you seen Pod, the owl?' asked Simon.

'I take it that you're talking about the unusual looking Blue Owl that was with you at breakfast. No, I haven't seen him.'

'He's been missing all morning,' said Simon, 'and we can't find him on the upper decks. We want to go down to search for him in the lower decks. He's old and may have got stuck somewhere. Will you tell us how to get down there?'

'The lower decks are private. And they're completely out of

bounds for passengers. I'll keep an eye out for him. But I have to warn you that there have been a lot of disappearances in these waters. We are crossing the Sea of Sorrows right now and passing very close to Eyrie Island. It's an evil place. Bad things are happening there. Your owl may have got mixed up with some of the eagles who come to spy on us. He may have had a mishap.'

'What kind of a mishap?' asked Simon.

'These waters are terribly dangerous,' said the cook.

'What do you mean?' asked Simon.

'Eyrie Island,' said the cook in a low voice. 'I know things about that island. Once it was a great place. There was an abbey there and lots of villages. Now the place is deserted. The waters are cursed and only eagles live there. It's ruled by their tyrant warlord.'

'Come on, Chef,' called the cook's assistant. 'We're finished here.'

'Keep searching,' said the chef to Simon, 'and I'll put the word out that the owl is missing. I promise you I'll search the lower decks myself.'

'But why aren't we allowed down to the lower decks and what's all the secrecy about?' asked Simon.

The chef stared hard at Simon, his lips firmly sealed.

'Chef, it's time to go,' persisted the assistant who was now standing inside the elevator.

'Now just you hold on!' demanded Simon. 'Take me to your captain, that's if there is a captain on this ship.'

'I'm not taking you anywhere, boy,' replied the head chef.

'And take a piece of my advice. Mind your own business or you'll find yourself under ship's arrest.'

The chef spun around and charged off through the elevator door. It slid shut and they heard the sound of it descending. Simon looked at Kerry in bewilderment. Suddenly, he clapped his hands.

'I have it,' he said and then lowered his voice. 'There's got to be a way into that elevator and down into the lower decks. All I have to do is find it and then I'll go down there and search for Pod myself.'

'You're not going down on your own,' said Kerry. 'I'll come with you. It was me who arranged this trip. And I don't want you getting arrested.'

❊❊❊

Timmy and Dot circled the ship and checked the portholes of the lower decks. They found no trace of Pod or the eagles. They were back waiting on the open air deck when Kerry and Simon returned from lunch.

'I'm so worried about poor old Pod,' said Kerry. 'This is my fault. He never wanted to come with us in the first place. And I talked him into coming on this trip. I'll never forgive myself if anything has happened to him.'

'Don't be a dope, Kerry,' said Simon. 'We all wanted to come on this trip. And we will find him. I've just got to find a way into that elevator. It's the only way down to the lower decks. I'm going back to the dining cabin now to check it out.'

Kerry hurried after him and watched as he examined the

walls around the elevator doors for switches and buttons. Then he searched under the food counter.

'There must be a way of calling that lift up,' said Simon.

'Maybe it's operated by remote control,' said Kerry. 'The cooks must have taken it with them.'

'What's this?' Simon asked, 'It looks like a tunnel of some kind.'

'That's the rubbish chute,' said Kerry. 'It's where they throw the waste food.'

'Perfect,' exclaimed Simon. 'I'm going down. I'll just about fit in there. You wait for me here. I won't be long.'

'But, Simon, this chute is not for humans. It's for waste food and plastic bags. You could get stuck on the way down or mangled in a shredding machine at the bottom.'

'OK I'll throw something down,' said Simon, rooting in his trouser pockets. He found a few coins and tossed them down the chute. They rustled as they hit the bottom.

'I don't hear any shredding machine,' said Simon.

'A few coins wouldn't be enough to set it off.'

Simon pulled a large bag of white serviettes out from under the counter. He pushed it down the rubbish chute and leaned in to watch it fall. It landed with a faint thud.

'I can still see the white serviette bag,' said Simon. 'There is no shredding machine.'

'Well, if you do go down that rubbish chute,' said Kerry, 'have you thought about how you're going to get back up here?'

'I'll come back in the elevator, of course.'

'But anything could happen to you, Simon.'

'I'm going down there, Kerry, whether you like it or not. Something has happened to Pod. And we're not going to find him talking about it up here. The only way to go is down.'

'I'm not letting you go on your own, Simon. If you go down there I'm coming with you. Just call me when you hit the bottom of the chute and I'll follow. If you're brave enough to go down that dirty, old chute then so am I.'

Simon squeezed into the rubbish chute. Kerry heard him sliding down and landing with a crunch at the bottom.

'Come on, Kerry,' his voice echoed. 'It's perfectly safe.'

Kerry followed him into the rubbish chute and let herself go. She felt the downward pull as she descended into the darkness of the ship. Finally, she hit the bottom with a soft thump. She had landed on a bed of rubbish bags and serviettes.

CHAPTER 6

Church Bells

'Come on, Kerry, let's get out of this rubbish dump,' said Simon.

Kerry scrambled off the large pile of rubbish bags under the chute. They had landed in a dark room with a crack of light coming in beneath the door. She was feeling a bit nervous now. What if they were discovered in the secret part of the ship? Would they be thrown overboard like in the pirate days, and forced to swim to Eyrie Island? Kerry shuddered at the thought. She was beginning to feel apprehensive about where this search for Pod was leading them.

'Kerry, are you alright?' asked Simon. 'Come on. If Pod is down here we'll find him.'

Kerry thought about her friend Pod, nervous and lost somewhere on the ship or, worse still, in the clutches of the Giant Eagles from Eyrie Island. She took a deep breath and prepared to follow Simon. He opened the door and stepped out of the rubbish room.

'All clear,' he said.

Kerry followed Simon out onto a long passageway. They stood at the end of the passage looking around them. Lanterns hung intermittently along the walls, casting a dim light down to the other end of the narrow corridor.

'We'd better hurry before someone finds us,' Kerry said in her bravest voice.

As they crept down the passageway Kerry heard the ship creak. There was a lack of fresh air in the passage. The vessel heaved against the waves outside and made her stomach lurch. A sudden chiming of bells, somewhere in the distance added to the mounting tension she felt. She wondered if this journey to the Land of Fire was a good idea after all. Perhaps she should have heeded Pod's warnings and stayed at home in Kilbeggin.

They reached the end of the passageway and found that it took a sharp right turn. The bells echoed louder as they crept cautiously around the corner.

'Why are those church bells ringing in the middle of the ocean?' whispered Kerry.

'Look straight ahead,' said Simon. 'It looks like we're approaching some kind of a chapel.'

They hurried on along the passageway until they came to the pointed arch. Here the walls rose to support a wooden vaulted ceiling that stretched before them towards a second arch. Under it stood two large, heavy, wooden doors. They paused for some moments gazing at the intricate images of biblical scenes delicately sculpted into the dark wood. The bells stopped ringing.

'This is Noah's Ark,' said Kerry, running her fingers over the carving. 'All these creatures were on board while it tossed in the waves during the great flood.'

Pictures of pairs of lions, elephants, tigers, snakes and birds of many kinds were carved into the dark wood.

'And look, that's Jonah in the mouth of the whale ready to be devoured.'

Somewhere below them the ship groaned. The bells started ringing again and Kerry felt faint. Simon pushed one of the doors open and pulled her through. They found themselves standing in dark shadows at the back of an ornate chapel. The sound of the bells came from directly above them and echoed around the walls. A long nave led to a marble altar decorated with elaborate golden statues. The aisles on both sides were lined with wooden carvings, crammed into niches and side altars.

'I don't understand it,' said Simon. 'This is a full-scale church, floating in the middle of the ocean.'

'And it's really old,' said Kerry. 'The wood carvings must have been brought here from a very ancient church.'

'Shhhh … I think I hear someone coming,' whispered Simon. 'Stand still.'

They stood in the shadows and listened as the footsteps approached. The sounds were coming from the very same door they had just entered. It opened and there stood a tall figure in a dark grey, hooded cloak. Kerry knew it was the man who had been attacked by the eagle in Kilbeggin. She couldn't see his face, which was hidden under the deep cowl of his cloak. Without looking left or right the man moved swiftly up the aisle and crossed the altar. Simon made a move to follow him but Kerry pulled him back. Then the man turned into a side altar and quickly disappeared out of sight.

Suddenly, the bells stopped ringing and a deep chanting floated towards them. A procession of monks wearing brown habits entered the church from behind the main altar. Each one carried a candle and a prayer book. They filed into the pews at the top of the church. The sound of the monks rhythmic chanting and the beauty of the church's stained-glass portholes and painted altars filled Kerry with a sense of awe.

At last the chanting stopped and the monks knelt to pray. It was then that Kerry felt they were being watched. She turned to see a pair of flashing green eyes staring at her through the dark shadows of the altar. She gasped loudly. Simon caught her by the arm. Some of the monks looked around at hearing the noise and one of them got up and began to shuffle towards them with his candle held high. The only way for Simon and Kerry to go was back in the direction they came from. They slipped through the tall wooden doors, ran through the archway and back down the corridor to the second arch. They stood into the shadow behind it. Nobody followed.

'Did you see those green eyes?' asked Kerry. 'Somebody was watching us in there. We've been seen.'

But before Kerry had a chance to say another word an enormous Giant Eagle stuck his beak over an archway and looked down on them with a cold, glassy stare.

Kerry and Simon froze. The eagle's large, pointed beak was almost touching their heads. He was over three feet tall with brown and golden feathers. His eyes were yellow. Leaning over, he looked at them sternly.

'No need to go any further,' the eagle ordered. 'I've got you covered. Now, what exactly are you doing snooping around here. This part of the ship is strictly private.'

'We're not snooping and we have a good reason for being here,' replied Simon.

'Let's hear it then,' commanded the eagle.

'Tell me who you are first,' said Simon.

'My name is Grinwick,' said the eagle, 'I'm a security guard on this ship and you shouldn't be down here. Only the monks are allowed in the lower decks. I'm placing you under arrest and bringing you before the Abbot. He will probably throw you into the ship's jail for trespassing on private property.'

'No, please don't,' pleaded Kerry. 'We were just looking for an owl. He is our friend and he has been missing all day. I'm very worried about him. We just thought he might have come down here hunting for rats. We don't want to disturb anyone.'

The eagle widened his golden eyes and stared at Kerry for a moment. 'Is this owl of yours an unusual shade of blue?'

'Oh yes. Have you seen him?'

'No. But I've heard what happened to him and unfortunately it's not good. The owl has been captured by Red Beak, King of the Giant Eagles, who lives on Eyrie Island.'

'What? Pod captured by the King of the Eagles! How do

you know?'

'I know about most things that go on over there. I once lived on Eyrie Island myself. It wasn't called Eyrie Island back then, before Red Beak and his army took it over. It was called the Isle of Dun Ruah. When Red Beak banished the monks from their abbey on the island, they took refuge on this ship. They gave the name of the island to their floating monastery. That's why this ship is called "The Ark of Dun Ruah".'

'Does this eagle – Red Beak – have red eyes that send out beams of light?' Simon asked.

'That's him. He's an evil bird. Those eyes see everything.'

'We saw him last night as we boarded the ship. He was up on the mast.'

'I knew it,' said Grinwick. 'There was something in the air last night, a terrible presence.'

'How do you know that Pod was captured?' Kerry asked.

'I have many friends and family on the island. Some of them keep me informed. There are many good eagles living out there still. They're forced to work for Red Beak against their will.'

'But what do they want with Pod?' said Simon. 'He's just a harmless old owl.'

'Feathers,' said Grinwick. 'That owl has beautiful bright blue feathers. They are very valuable. Eagles love them. I've heard that Red Beak is planning to make himself and his Queen a pair of matching royal-blue cloaks. He's been searching for the perfect shade of blue feathers for years. Your owl has got them. He's flown straight into their clutches. And when Red Beak's got his first pair of cloaks finished, he'll make more of them to export to Royal Eagle families all over the world. That's how he operates. He's greedy. He loves an opportunity to make money and blue feathers are more valuable than diamonds to the Royal Eagles.'

'When he's got enough feathers, will he let Pod go?' asked Kerry.

Grinwick laughed.

'He'll never have enough feathers! They tell me that Red Beak is developing some formula. He plans to inject it into the owl to make him grow more feathers and then he'll pluck him alive. After that he'll wait for your friend Pod to grow another crop so he can keep harvesting them.'

'This is an outrage. He won't get away with this,' exclaimed Simon. 'We've got to get onto the island. And we have to get there now. We need a boat. You must have an inflatable one on board or we could take one of the lifeboats.'

'It's not as simple as that,' said Grinwick.

'But Pod will have a nervous breakdown if they pluck his feathers.'

'Red Beak is a dangerous warlord. He is a dictator and capable of terrible cruelty. You don't know what you're getting into. My advice to you is to keep out of Red Beak's way.'

'But what about poor old Pod? We can't leave him alone on a deserted island with some crazy eagle warlord.'

'I could tell you many terrible things about Eyrie Island. But it's a long story. And I don't want to waste any more time talking here. I have a duty to report you to the Abbot. You must accompany me to his quarters right now.'

CHAPTER 7

Grinwick

Kerry and Simon were escorted by Grinwick, the Giant Eagle, through a series of narrow passageways. They emerged out onto a small, open air deck. A rugged island was clearly visible from where they stood looking out over the sea. It had three peaks and was surrounded by jagged cliffs. It looked grey and desolate. Grinwick knocked on a cabin door with his sharp beak. There was no reply.

'The Abbot must be at vespers,' said Grinwick, 'and he doesn't like to be disturbed during prayer time so we'll have to wait.'

'That must be Eyrie Island,' said Simon, gazing out across the waves. 'It looks like a bleak sort of place.'

'Yes and you can just see the Abbey from here between those two jagged peaks at the eastern end of the island. That's where Red Beak lives with his Queen.'

'What was it like when you lived there?'

'Oh, it was beautiful back when I was young,' said Grinwick. 'At that time it was a peaceful island well known for its learning and the writings of the ancient monks. My father was a friend of the chief of the island, Coleman Cooley. He was a good leader and a kind and wise man. He came from a long line of fair and just chieftains. His descendents live on the island to this day. Now, of course, they've been banished from their towns and villages and forced into the caves by the Giant Eagles.'

'But you're a Giant Eagle too,' said Simon.

'Yes, I'm a Giant Eagle and proud of it. Most Giant Eagles are quiet creatures who live in seclusion. We lived for centuries in harmony with the islanders. That is until Red Beak came along.'

'I thought that Giant Eagles were extinct.'

'Many people think we're extinct but we've survived, hidden in the huge rock crevices on the island. We have always got on well with the people there. In fact, the people were very good to us and protected us from the outside world.'

'So what happened to Red Beak?' asked Simon.

'When I was a chick, the Giant Eagle population on the island started to grow. Red Beak was a fledgling but even at a young age he was greedy for power. He started creating mischief on the island. He attacked the farming community, raided their fields and destroyed their crops.'

'But why didn't anyone stop him?' said Kerry.

'Coleman Cooley, the chieftain, was such a peaceful man that he did little to stop Red Beak. I suppose he never believed that an eagle could gain control of the island. As the years went by Red Beak grew in power. He terrorised the islanders and the monks who lived in the Abbey. Most of the people got fed up with the situation. They gathered their possessions and emigrated. Those who stayed fled to the massive underground cave system on the island. I've heard that they've built a town down there at the edge of an underground lake.'

'And what happened to the monks?' Kerry asked.

'Finally, the monks had to leave the island too. After that, Red Beak crowned himself king. Later he discovered that another eagle colony existed on a southern island called Iolathar. He went there to visit and returned with his bride, Kiki. She was crowned queen and they made the Abbey their palace. Since then he has ruled the island in a reign of terror. He has raised an army of vicious hit men. He is capable of turning against his own most loyal friends on a whim. None of them are safe. I have many friends and even family members working for Red Beak against their will. They live in constant fear for their lives.'

'But why don't they stand up to him?' asked Simon.

'It's not easy. Red Beak has got squadrons of secret police. Nobody knows exactly who they are. They spy on members of their own families and turn their friends in if they don't agree with Red Beak's policies. Then they're thrown in prison where they are tortured and brainwashed into Red Beak's philosophy.'

'What is his philosophy?' Kerry asked.

'Eagle Power,' said Grinwick. 'Red Beak claims to have

supernatural powers. He says his eyes can see through walls. He wants to raise up a tribe of Giant Eagle descendants who have powers like him and who will rule the world.'

'Eagle Power,' cried Simon. 'He's crazy if he thinks a bunch of eagles are going to take over the world. Is nobody going to stop him?'

'It's not that simple. His spies and secret police tell him who is about to betray him. They know everything. They also keep control of the seas around the island. Many people call it the Sea of Sorrows. Only eagles are allowed to cross over to the island. Passing ships often lose passengers who get lured into the whispering waves. They disappear forever.'

'What happened to the chief of the island and his family?' Kerry asked.

'They say that Coleman Cooley and his wife and son were murdered by Red Beak, along with most of his family and chief officials.'

'But that's terrible. Red Beak is truly wicked. And I feel so sorry for the poor monks. It must be awful to be banished from their towns and villages to this floating monastery for the rest of their lives.'

'Well it's supposed to be a secret,' said Grinwick. 'The monks want to keep it that way. They don't mingle with the passengers. They live down here in the hull of the ship and take paying passengers to support themselves. The money is also used to help the cave dwellers on the island. They often deliver food and clothes to them on the lifeboats at night-time. But, of course, the monks hope to go back to the island and reclaim their monastery. We all pray that someday a great leader will come to face Red Beak and his cronies and break his tyranny over Eyrie Island.'

'What I can't understand about all this is why Pod's feathers are so valuable,' said Simon. 'Nobody has ever come looking for his feathers before.'

'Feathers are very valuable to Giant Eagles,' said Grinwick, 'especially such rare, royal-blue feathers! Red Beak's wife, Kiki, is very beautiful. But she is a vain and proud creature. She comes from a royal family of Great Eagles. To gain her hand in marriage Red Beak convinced her family that he has true blue blood in his veins. They believe that he ascended as an heir to the throne of the Kingdom of Eyrie Island. He told them nothing about his wicked coup. He'll be hoping that the royal-blue feathered cloaks will keep his wife happy. Then he'll give cloaks as gifts to her family. He is constantly looking for an opportunity to impress them and to keep his Queen at his side. Many times she has threatened to leave him. The ruling couple are well known for their tempestuous relationship and their frequent arguments.'

'We've got to do something fast,' said Simon.

'No, you will stay here until the Abbot comes back,' ordered Grinwick. 'He will be the one to decide what should be done.'

'It may be too late by the time the Abbot comes back,' argued Simon.

'Yes Grinwick, you've got to help us,' pleaded Kerry. 'It's your island and your loved ones that are being controlled by that brainwashing Eagle King. How long are you going to let this go on for?'

Grinwick sighed. 'You don't know what you're getting into. Red Beak has five thousand dangerous and vicious eagles in his army. You don't want to tangle with them. It's time to forget about your friend Pod. Maybe Red Beak will let him go as soon as he's got enough feathers.'

'I'm not letting those savages pluck poor old Pod alive,' said Simon, shaking his fist in the air. 'He'd never survive it. I will not leave here without him.'

'Shhhh! Keep your voice down,' said Grinwick. 'I've told you that Red Beak has his spies everywhere.'

'Well how would you feel if you were plucked alive?' challenged Simon.

Grinwick hung his head and was at a loss for something to say.

'I'm not afraid of Red Eagle or Red Beak or whatever you call him,' cried Simon. 'I'm going over there myself to face that eagle and get Pod back. He'll be sorry when I'm through with him. I'm going to swim across. I can easily make it from here. It's quite close.'

Simon had already jumped onto the railings and was preparing to dive.

'No,' said Grinwick. 'The waters are treacherous. You'll never survive. And I will try to help you. I'm working for the Abbot. He's a good and wise man and I believe he's got a plan to deal with Red Beak. Wait and talk to him. Vespers will be over in two hours.'

'I'm not sitting around here for another two hours. Now is

the time to deal with Red Beak before anyone else around here goes missing!'

'Wait! Wait! I'll carry you to the island.'

'What?'

'There's a strong sea breeze blowing towards the island today. I can carry you there.'

'Then you'll have to take me too,' said Kerry.

'OK, OK. But first I'll take Simon. You wait here,' said Grinwick.

He flew up and grasped Simon's shoulders firmly in his mighty claws. Lifting him high into the air, he soared out over the Sea of Sorrows. Kerry marvelled at the size of the bird as he flew. She figured that he must have a wingspan of at least seven feet. She saw him drop Simon on a sandy beach in the distance and then return to the ship.

Before she knew it Kerry herself was in the eagle's clutches, gliding high over the blue sea, looking down over the whispering waves. Soon they reached Eyrie Island. She saw that it had a rugged coastline and many tall cliffs. At one end of the island two jagged peaks were visible rising up from a lofty mountain range. The Abbey lay nestled in the foothills between them. A single peak dominated the other end of the island. The beauty of the view from beneath the eagle's wings took Kerry's breath away.

Grinwick flew low over a long, cliff-lined, sandy beach and began his descent. He dropped her beside Simon who was keeping out of sight under a shaded rock face. The eagle led them to a narrow crevice in the tall cliff. They climbed through and inside found a long tunnel, which wound its way through the rock. Simon struck a match and lifted it over their heads. Kerry could see that the tunnel was deep and wide and glistening in dark red marble. Water dripped from a domed ceiling into still pools along the path. Grinwick led them through a series of lofty caverns all banded in glimmering red and white marble.

'This is amazing,' said Simon.

'It is an ancient underground route to the Abbey,' said Grinwick.

'Did you say that the island has a massive cave system?' Kerry asked.

'Yes, the entire island is a warren of natural caves of great beauty. There has been a tradition of people living in the caves going back to ancient times. But we eagles generally keep away from the caves. We can only use the widest ones. Most of us are terrified of enclosed spaces. We were born to live in the air, not underground. And this is as far as I can go.'

Grinwick had paused at a narrow point in a long cavern. Its floor sloped steeply downwards.

'Where are we?' asked Simon.

Grinwick pointed at a jagged crack in the rock at the end of the cave.

'Go through and you will find a passage that will take you to the Abbey, the home of the Great Red Beaked Eagle,' whispered Grinwick. 'This is where I leave you. Keep going straight ahead and you will come to some cellars. Go through them and you'll find a stairs that will lead you straight to Red

Beak's Great Hall. Now I must go. I've taken enough risk by just bringing you here. I wish you Godspeed. And I hope you find your friend the owl. I will return now to tell the Abbot that I brought you here. Perhaps he will send the Messenger to help you.'

'What messenger?' Simon asked.

'The Messenger ... haven't you heard of him?'

Simon and Kerry shook their heads.

'They say that the Messenger comes from an ancient and distant realm. He has great power and has always been a guardian and protector of the monks. It is widely held that he has walked the earth since the dawn of time.'

'Since the dawn of time!' exclaimed Simon.

'Yes. Many don't believe in the Messenger. But I have seen him with my own eyes. I've heard that the Abbot has been talking to him in recent times. There are fresh hopes that he will break the tyranny of Red Beak and his henchmen. But now I must hurry. Let me warn you again that Red Beak is dangerous. There's no limit to his trickery.'

'Please do us one favour,' said Kerry. 'Will you tell our friends the swiftails that we are here? And ask them to follow us. They are waiting for us on the top deck of the Ark of Dun Ruah.'

Grinwick nodded and left them. Kerry and Simon were alone under the great Abbey of Eyrie Island.

CHAPTER 8

Kerry and Simon in the Abbey

Kerry and Simon made their way through a chain of narrow tunnels until they found themselves in the musty cellars of the Abbey. They came to a heavy wooden door that Simon pushed open. Beyond it stood a narrow staircase. They climbed the stairs to a large cellar filled with caskets of wine. At the end of the cellar stood a wide staircase that was flooded with shafts of natural light, falling from above.

'Follow the light,' said Simon.

They crept up the long staircase, into the brightness, through a vaulted hallway that led straight to an open door. Kerry and Simon stood looking through the doorway into a magnificent dining hall adorned with dazzling chandeliers.

'I expect this must have been the place where the monks ate their daily meals,' said Kerry, 'and now it's been converted into a great banquet hall.'

A huge ornate fireplace stood before her on the opposite

wall. There was an arched doorway on her right. Narrow windows, placed high up on the stone walls above the doorway let shafts of coloured light through their stained glass. The room was also lit by small crystal lamps, recessed in little alcoves. Two high thrones stood side by side on the left side of the room. They were very elaborately carved and gilded in glittering gold. The room was filled with dark wooden furniture and the walls hung with tapestries.

'What a stunning room!' Kerry exclaimed. 'It looks more like a palace than an abbey.'

They crossed the room and stood before the two large thrones.

'These are perches for eagles,' said Simon pointing at a metal bar on each seat.

'The largest throne must be for Red Beak. The smaller one is for his wife.'

The sound of flapping wings brought their inspection of the room to an abrupt end. A breeze blew up the dust around them. It was coming from the open doorway through which they had entered. Simon scanned the room for somewhere to hide. A small door near the fireplace caught his eye. Grabbing Kerry by the arm, he rushed over and opened the door. They slipped through it and quietly closed the door behind them.

Kerry and Simon hurried down a stone corridor towards a descending staircase. When they reached the bottom they found a little scullery and off it stood a large kitchen. Just as they were about to enter it they heard the sound of some creature shuffling around inside. There was a clatter of dishes and then the sound of voices.

'Hurry up with the owl's lunch,' said a voice, 'And give him plenty to eat. Red Beak has sent orders to fatten him up.'

'It's nearly ready,' replied another voice. 'I'll take it straight down to the dungeons, sir.'

'Then get a move on!'

More shuffling sounds came from the kitchen and then a door slammed.

'After him,' whispered Simon.

They darted into the kitchen and through a door at the other end. They could hear the eagle scratching the floor ahead of them with his sharp claws as he moved down the corridor. Simon and Kerry followed him to a stone stairway and descended it into a dark passage.

Now they heard sounds approaching them from behind.

'Quick, get behind those bags,' said Simon, pulling Kerry behind some soft brown sacks stacked high on the passage floor. They crouched down behind them.

Scraping and scratching sounds echoed across the floor. Heavy and raspy breathing filled the air. Another door was slammed. Kerry felt a sweat breaking out on her forehead as the scratching sounds moved closer. Suddenly, she felt a cold rush of air above her head. She looked up and screamed.

A Giant Eagle hovered above them. He was peering down at them with searing red eyes.

'Run,' cried Simon. He picked up a brown sack and threw it at the eagle. The bag burst as it hit the bird and smothered it in flour. The stunned eagle fell to the floor in a great cloud of white dust. There was nowhere for Kerry and Simon to go but back up the stairs. They could hear the eagle screaming behind them.

They rushed on back to the kitchen and into the corridor beyond it. In her hurry, Kerry panicked. She lost her footing on the old flagstone floor and tumbled headlong into a hanging tapestry. To her shock, it gave way. She fell through the tapestry and landed on the floor of a small, dark room. Simon followed close behind her. He pulled the tapestry back into place behind them. They retreated from the doorway into a dark corner and crouched silently in the shadows.

Then they heard the sound of a great flapping of wings along the corridor and the echoes of eagles crying out. With a powerful rush of wind they felt the surge of a great flock of eagles passing the tapestry door. Kerry and Simon waited until the sounds died down.

It was evident that the room in which they found themselves was once a monk's cell. It was small and bare with whitewashed walls and a simple flagstone floor. Above them were dark wooden beams. A single window was set high up under the ceiling, way above their heads. It let a narrow shaft of light into the room. Simon climbed up onto the only piece of furniture in the room, a tall wooden table. From here he jumped onto the window ledge. He opened the window and looked out.

'It's just big enough for us to get through,' he said, 'but you'll have to climb up here to the window, Kerry. We can run across those lawns and find cover under the trees beyond. Come up and see for yourself.'

Kerry tried to climb onto the table. She whimpered in pain.

'I think I've twisted my ankle.'

'Take my hand.'

She took Simon's hand and tried to climb up to the window ledge beside him.

'It's no use Simon. My ankle is killing me. I can't climb up. The place is probably crawling with guards and it won't be long before they'd catch up with me out there. You'll have a better chance of making it to the trees on your own.'

'I can't leave you here alone,' said Simon.

'But I should be safe in here. I don't think the eagles can come into this room. The doorway looks too narrow. Remember Grinwick saying the eagles hate enclosed spaces? And I now know that Pod is somewhere down that dark passage where we saw the eagle. It must lead to the dungeons. I want to stay near him. When things quieten down, I'll go and look for him again. You go and get help.'

'I'll have a look outside,' said Simon, 'to see if the coast is clear. Then I'll be straight back to get you out. I'll carry you if I have to.'

'No, Simon, I'd only slow you down,' said Kerry. 'You've got to get help. Find some of the islanders and raise the alarm. It's our only chance.'

'I'll be back as soon as I can,' said Simon. 'I promise you Red Beak won't get away with what he is doing on this island. Kerry, you've got to be brave. Stay in this room and I'll be back for you as soon as it's safe. And here, take these. You will need them if you go looking for Pod.'

Simon produced a large box of matches from the depths of one of his pockets. He placed them in Kerry's hands.

'Remember, the green ones are for fire and the white ones for light. Eagles hate fire. So if you meet one, be sure to use the matches. Hide them in your jacket.'

'Don't be long,' said Kerry.

She watched Simon's legs disappear through the window. The cries of eagles rose in the distance. The light coming from the window faded as the skies darkened.

❁❁❁

A sharp hissing startled Kerry. She had a horrible feeling that she wasn't alone in the room. She looked around at the bare walls. The room seemed empty. But she could feel something breathing close to her skin. She edged towards the tapestry. The hissing started again. It was louder now and seemed to be coming from the ceiling. Kerry trembled. She felt she was trapped in a room with some horrible creature. She pulled back the tapestry and limped out into the corridor. A hideous cackle broke out above her. She looked upwards and found herself staring straight into two piercing red eyes. They bored right through her insides, chilling her to the bone. Then she saw the long, protruding red beak, which curved into a mean-looking hook. She screamed in horror but then the eagle leaned his long neck forward and gave a deep and menacing sneer.

'So you thought you could hide from me, did you? Nothing escapes Great Red Beak, King of the Eagles.'

The creature was at least four feet tall with grey and gold feathers. His breast was a paler shade of grey tinged with red flecks. Huge yellow claws curled around the ledge above the doorway. On one of his claws he wore a ring with a large dazzling sapphire. 'You and your brother have been prowling around my palace,' snarled Red Beak. 'Did you think you'd get away with that? Nothing, absolutely nothing, goes on in my palace without my knowing it, do you hear?'

The eagle's red eyes bored through her. Kerry retreated towards the tapestry. She looked back at the tiny room searching for a way out, but a strong eagle guard stood behind her and barred her way.

'Don't even think about escaping. My guards have you surrounded. There's no way out for you. And that brother of yours won't get far either. My guards are after him. You are all alone on my island without a hope of escape. And tears will do you no good. I have absolutely no sympathy for emotional outbursts!'

'You won't get away with this,' said Kerry, finding her voice in her rage against the monster that ranted before her. She could feel his cold breath on her face.

He fluffed up his feathers.

'You try to sound brave but I can see through you. And I know you have come all this way to look for your friend, the Blue Owl. Well, he's safely locked up in an iron cage, which has been welded shut and cannot be opened. I think he's feeling a bit lonely. I want him to be happy so he'll produce a beautiful crop of feathers for me. So I'm going to put you into another iron cage beside him in the dungeons, to keep him company. As you can see, this has worked out perfectly for me as, of course, everything does.'

'Don't be so sure,' interrupted Kerry, her angry eyes flashing at the eagle. A new fire in her heart gave her the courage to tackle him. 'My friends know I am here on Eyrie Island. They'll come looking for me.'

Red Beak gave her an icy glare.

'You don't know what you are dealing with, you stupid child. Guards, seize her. Take her and lock her up in the dungeons.'

By now a flock of twenty eagles had surrounded Kerry and one of them grabbed her shoulders in his long claws. Swiftly he lifted her up into the air. They flew down a long corridor and through a maze of passages. Finally, they arrived in the dungeons.

Pod let out a loud hoot when he saw Kerry. He flew at the bars of his cage trying to break free. To Kerry's relief, the Blue Owl was still in one piece. His full coat of feathers seemed to be intact.

They flung Kerry into a cage beside him. Then one of the guards produced a blow torch. He sealed the cage door shut and checked that it was secure. The flock departed the dungeon, slamming its great wooden door behind them. Kerry heard the key turn in the lock.

CHAPTER 9

Simon goes Underground

Simon climbed through the Abbey window into the bright sunshine. He stood transfixed as he gazed at the most beautiful garden he had ever seen. A wide pathway of shimmering white pebbles led to silver gates in the distance. Flowers of red and yellow lined the pathway. On either side, cascading fountains plunged into large blue ponds. The perimeter of the garden was planted with trees and shrubs, which ran up to the great walls of the Abbey.

A loud cackling sound rose from inside the Abbey behind him. He turned to see the door of the Abbey burst open. Dozens of eagles soared up into the sky. Simon knew they were looking for him. He searched for somewhere to hide. Running towards the trees, he spotted a gate in the Abbey wall and got through it. Before him, there stretched dense woodlands.

The screaming cries of flocks of eagles were getting louder. Simon looked back to see a dark cloud of eagles flying over the Abbey wall. They were making straight for him through the trees.

'I've got to find cover,' he muttered as he searched for someplace to hide.

Simon ran for the undergrowth. He knew that the eagles had seen him and were closing in. If he was caught there would be no hope for Kerry and Pod. They would all be trapped in the Abbey and be at the mercy of Red Beak and his minions. Simon sensed that the woods behind him were thick with eagle flocks hunting him down. They were closing in fast.

'There he is,' he heard an eagle cry. There was no escape. Desperately, he plunged deeper into the undergrowth. Then the ground gave way. He fell.

'Wooooaaaaa …'

Down, down, down. Simon fell through a deep, dark hole in the ground. On and on he went until he realised that his body was touching the sides of a steep shaft. Careering downwards at top speed, his heart raced. The sides of the shaft were smooth and he sped onwards deep into the earth. Then he landed with a heavy thump on what felt like a soft bed of leaves. He sat for a moment in total darkness wondering if he was dead or alive. A gentle breeze cooled his face and the faint sound of trickling water stirred him to life. Simon reached inside his jacket and rooted around for one of his many boxes of matches. He fished out a long, narrow match and struck it. To his relief it flared into a bright beam of light. He looked around and gasped.

'It's a labyrinth of caves!'

Simon stared in amazement at the glistening walls that surrounded him. He could see little waterfalls cascading down one end of the cave while the gnarled roots of old trees twisted around the other walls in interwoven patterns. The waterfalls flowed into a pond, which joined a stream and disappeared into an enormous white marbled archway leading on to other caverns beyond. Simon got to his feet and started following the stream. He went through the arch and on into a lofty chamber of sheer white marble, keeping to a narrow ledge just above the water level. Many other caves and passages branched off this one.

'If I stay beside the stream,' Simon reasoned, 'it will lead me towards the sea, where I can try to find help.'

The stream gradually grew wider and the ledge he trod on became narrower. He was afraid that the ledge would become too narrow to balance on and that he would have to turn away from the watercourse.

Suddenly, he came upon a boat. It was sitting on a tiny ledge that appeared just below the ledge he walked on. The boat was old, with the paint falling off but it looked intact. Simon jumped down to the lower ledge and hauled the little boat into the water, testing it for any sign of leaks. It had no oars and there were none to be found anywhere around it. But it looked dry and solid. He stepped into the boat and let it drift down the stream.

As the boat moved forward the stream broadened into a river. Other streams fed it from adjoining channels and it began to pick up speed. In the distance he became aware of a gurgling sound and a loud swishing of water. The boat moved swiftly as a current began to gather. Before he could think of a way to steer it to safety the boat was in the centre of the rushing current.

'It's out of control,' Simon gasped. 'I've got to hang on to this boat or I'm done for. And I'll do it if it takes every ounce of strength I've got left!'

The boat rushed on down a long, narrow tunnel and through more caves. The roar of water was almost deafening as it plunged through a huge circular cave. To his horror, Simon saw that the boat was skirting around the edge of a whirlpool.

'Help, someone help me!' Simon shouted over the noise of the rushing water.

He was swirling around the whirlpool faster now and getting dangerously close to the centre. He knew that when he hit the eye of the whirlpool the boat would be pulled under with the strength of the current. Simon realised he was now in serious trouble. The boat was falling apart. Bits of painted wood flew everywhere.

Simon felt his legs being pulled down as the water sucked him under. He was dragged underwater with the torrential current until he felt himself being flung to the bottom of the pool. He had a terrible urge to breathe but he held on, dying for air and hoping that he would be released from the great surge of water. Just when he thought he couldn't bear it any longer, his body rose to the surface and he gasped for air.

'Oh my God,' he roared.

He was quickly pulled down again with another rushing

current. The second time he came up he sensed that the water was flowing less urgently. He kept his head above water for several breaths.

He was approaching a low archway in the tunnel. Quickly he dived underwater and when he came up he saw another arch straight ahead. He took one deep breath before ducking again. When he surfaced, he saw a glimmer of light at the end of the tunnel. The roar of tumbling water was deafening. He knew that there must be a huge waterfall ahead.

Again Simon felt the tug of the current as it picked up speed. Dazzling shafts of light blinded his eyes. The end of the tunnel was in sight.

The roaring waterfall grew even louder. It was unbearable. Over the edge he sailed into dazzling light going into free fall with thousands of tons of water plummeting down behind him.

CHAPTER 10

Pod's Story

Red Beak's guards flew off leaving Kerry alone with Pod in the dungeon. A single candle lit the grey stone walls that glistened with dampness. The cell was a small, musty room with a sturdy wooden door. Clumps of straw were scattered around the floor. Sitting in her large, iron cage, Kerry waited for the sounds of the eagles to fade away. Pod stared at her with his huge, unblinking amber eyes. His breathing was laboured. And his thick crop of royal-blue feathers were standing on end.

'Oh, Pod. Thank God you're alive,' she whispered. 'Did they hurt you?'

'Hurt me?' said Pod. 'Those eagles have been torturing me all day with their mind games and their evil injections. I've got a terrible headache and my body is aching all over. But how on earth did you find me here?'

Kerry told Pod about how she, Simon and the swiftails had searched the ship for him. She told him about finding the rubbish chute and the chapel in the depths of the ship, about meeting Grinwick and him carrying them across the sea to the Abbey. Then she asked Pod to tell his story.

'When I left you in the dining cabin this morning,' he said, 'I went off to find something to eat for my breakfast. I hunted over the entire Ark of Dun Ruah for a rat or a mouse but I couldn't find a bite to eat. It's a very strange ship. All the lower decks were closed off. Even the portholes were locked. Then I got so hungry that I flew out over the seawaters and scooped a few sardines out of the waves. Of course, I was exhausted after being up all night listening to those eerie voices calling from the sea and trying not to fall under their spell. I guessed that the sea was enchanted and I wanted to come back to warn you about it. But I could see that you were still having your breakfast in the dining cabin. I saw Timmy and Dot flying high over the waves. Just looking at them made me feel exhausted and I got a terrible urge to fall asleep.'

'Yes, I heard those voices too,' said Kerry. 'I was dreaming all night about voices coming from the sea, about Simon getting lost and meeting the evil Eagle King. The awful thing is that most of it has come true. Did they abduct you when you fell asleep then?'

'Well, I looked around for a safe place to have a little nap and I found a porthole low down on the ship's side. It had a very deep ledge, which kept me shaded from the sun and was very private. So I decided to have a quick snooze with one eye open, like this.'

Pod paused to tilt his head to one side. He closed one of his large amber eyes. Then he let out a long snore.

'Pod, are you awake?' Kerry asked. 'Pod, wake up!'

'What? Oh where was I?' he said, opening his second eye with some effort.

'You said that you fell asleep in the porthole.'

'I know. Well, when I woke up there was a large swell in the sea and the ship was tossing. The waters became choppy and the waves were beating dangerously close to my ledge. I tried to fly out of my porthole without being lashed by the breakers but I lost my balance and went tumbling down into the water. It all happened so fast that I didn't have time to spread my wings. Then a huge wave hit me hard and dragged me underwater. The blow stunned me so much that I couldn't see straight. Then another wave pulled me way out to sea and far away from the ship. I tried to get out of the water but showers of sea spray and foam swirled over me and then a heavy mist came down. I lost sight of the Ark of Dun Ruah. It was then that I really started to panic.'

'It's not like you to fall asleep like that, Pod. You must have been exhausted.'

'I was. And it took a huge effort to gather my wits about me. Eventually, I managed to take flight. I tried to find a way to fly out of the mist but it was dark and thick. The more I tried to get out of the mist the more disorientated I became. I was terrified out there all alone above the whispering waters.'

'Poor Pod,' said Kerry. 'You must have lost your sense of direction.'

'We owls are experts at finding our way in the dark, but all my navigational instincts deserted me out there on the enchanted seas. There must be a terrible curse on those waters. It confused me so much that I guess I was flying around in circles. But after what seemed like ages the mist cleared a little and I saw a group of Giant Eagles above me. They looked very like the same Giant Eagles that were stalking me in Kilbeggin. Before I could get away they descended into my flight path and surrounded me. They didn't attack but they kept staring at me and asking me questions, moving closer and closer.'

'You must have been terrified.'

'I was so desperate that I answered all their questions. I told them I was lost and was looking for my way back to the Ark of Dun Ruah. The eagles whispered among themselves and then one of them said, "It just so happens that we are looking for the Ark of Dun Ruah ourselves. You can follow us." So I followed those eagles for a very long time. And I was sure that they were the same eagles who had been pestering me in Kilbeggin. I knew that they were leading me in the wrong direction but what choice had I but to follow them? They had me surrounded.'

'So they led you here.'

'Well, I tried to make a getaway first. I noticed that every now and then the eagles left me unguarded and grouped together to have a chat among themselves. During one of their conflabs I took the opportunity to escape by shooting upwards into the heavens as fast as I could soar. But they were on my tail straight away. Eagles are good at high altitudes. The leader of the flock seized me by the neck, with his long claws and the rest of the eagles closed in tight around me. They dragged me across the sea to the coast of this island. We flew over high cliffs and forests until we reached the foothills of the two peaks. Then I saw the Abbey below us. We entered it and flew through a maze of corridors and passages until they dumped me here in this awful dungeon.'

'Did you meet Red Beak himself?' Kerry asked.

'Yes. After a few hours the guards came to tell me that their King wished to meet me. I was escorted to the Great Eagle's private chambers. When he arrived he was surrounded by a bunch of tough-looking bodyguards. By that time I was so shattered that I couldn't speak.'

'Oh, Pod,' said Kerry. 'What did you think of him?'

'I think he looks more like a vulture than a Giant Eagle,' said Pod. 'He got his bodyguards to drag me onto a high perch in the centre of the room and then he circled around me examining my feathers. All the time he made horrible hissing sounds and his hooded red beady eyes almost burned through my body. Then he spoke to me. "You have very unusual feathers," said he, "My wife, Kiki, will carry out another examination on you in the morning. I'm sure she will be quite satisfied with them." He put me under the charge of his chief bodyguard, Roddick, and left. After that, Roddick and the guards started pushing me around. They forced me back up on the high perch and started poking me with their sharp claws. I was shaking so badly that I got a dose of the hiccups and toppled off. They all laughed and teased me as I fluttered around trying to regain my balance. Then I lost my temper.

"'Can someone explain to me why I've been kidnapped?" I yelled. "Why are you persecuting me like this? You're making a big mistake!"

"'No mistake at all," said Roddick. "The King is very pleased with you. Your feathers are a magnificent shade of royal blue and will be perfect for Queen Kiki's royal cloak. She will be delighted with you in the morning."

"'What?" I cried. "You're planning to strip me of my feathers to make a cloak. Are you completely mad?"

"'Well, we certainly didn't bring you here for your brains!" laughed Roddick. "What a pathetic little bird you are, falling off your perch and hiccuping all over the floor. You deserve to get a good plucking!"

"'I won't allow you to pluck me alive!"

"'You have no choice in the matter. And we'll pluck you whatever way we please – dead or alive! Tonight and tomorrow morning you will be injected with a special feather-growing formula. Then the Palace Plucker will be called to pluck every one of your blue feathers, one by one. Wait until you see his huge tweezers. It's a sharp-looking instrument! He'll pluck you until you are completely bald and before you get a chance to lick your wounds, we'll inject you with more feather-growing formula and pluck you all over again. You can look forward to a long life of plucking."

"'Wait till all my friends hear of this. They'll put a stop to this!"

"'If anyone comes here trying to rescue you, they'll get similar treatment. That tweezers can be used on human hair too. There's nothing like a slow and painful plucking to teach someone a lesson. Very effective!" he said.

'After they had another good laugh, Roddick ordered the guards to take me back to my cage in the dungeon. He said he would send down the injection later and that he'd have me nice and fat and fluffy in no time.'

'Poor Pod,' said Kerry when he had finished his story. 'What rotten, nasty beasts!'

'Yes, and the guards keep telling me how painful the plucking is going to be. We've got to get out of here, Kerry.'

'What are we going to do without Simon?' said Kerry. 'I hope they haven't caught him too. Do you think he got away safely?'

'He's not dead,' said Pod. 'I'd feel it in my bones if he was. We've got to believe he's alive and that he'll get us out of here. He's our only chance.'

The sound of flapping wings announced the return of the eagle guards. The key was turned in the lock and the cell door opened. A flock of eagles flew in carrying two bowls of strange-smelling liquid and a very large blue injection.

Two of the guards held Pod down while a third injected him in the neck. The horrified owl uttered a terrible cry. He stood trembling with all his blue feathers standing on end.

A bowl of yellowish broth with three large, green things floating around inside it was left outside Kerry's cage. She was handed a spoon to feed herself with, through the iron bars.

'What's this?' she cried.

'Turnip and brussels sprout soup,' said one of the guards.

'Yuck!' shouted Kerry.

'You're lucky to be getting anything at all. You're a trespasser. Breaking and entering, that's a serious crime on Eyrie Island. And as for you, Owl, his majesty has ordered that you will be plucked first thing tomorrow morning.'

'What?' Pod exclaimed. His eyes started to twitch. 'But I'm not ready.'

The guards laughed and one of them remarked, 'Of course you'll be ready. I can see the effect of those injections already. Your feathers are coming along very nicely. We'll be here bright and early tomorrow morning to take you to the Palace Plucker. So make sure you get your beauty sleep.'

The guards flew off tittering and jeering.

'See you tomorrow for feather plucking,' they cried, slamming the door.

It was a long night in the cold, dreary dungeon. Kerry tried to sleep on her cramped bed of straw but her feet kept getting stuck between the iron bars. Pod paced up and down his cage scratching and moaning. Some time in the early hours, Pod's hooting roused Kerry from her restless dreams. He was panicking.

'I'm going to be tortured in a few hours time. I've got to get out of here,' he cried.

Clinging to the iron bars of his cage, and rattling them with all his strength, Pod desperately tried to force the door open.

'I'm so hot and sweaty in these feathers and I'm getting fatter and heavier every second.'

Kerry studied him.

'Your feathers are growing thicker. You must have at least three times the amount of feathers you had when you arrived here.'

'I think I'm going to melt,' moaned Pod.

'Melt!' echoed Kerry gazing through the iron bars of her cage.

'Pod, you've just given me an idea. I think I have a way for us to escape.'

CHAPTER 11

A Maze and a Waterfall

Kerry gripped the iron bars of her cage, deep in the dark, musty dungeon. She stared intently at Pod, who was growing more feathers by the minute. Kerry's eyes were bright with excitement.

'Pod, you've just given me a great idea. I'm going to light a fire and melt some of those bars on your cage. Simon gave me some of his matches before he left me in the Abbey. I had totally forgotten about them. He told me that the green matches were for fire and the white ones are for light. I think one of them might come in very handy right now.'

'Simon's matches, are you crazy? They're disastrous. They never work the way he says they will. We could blow ourselves up!'

'But he's done a lot of work on improving them.'

'You've got to be joking Kerry. You'd actually use Simon's matches after all the accidents he's had? Remember all the times you had to ring the fire brigade. I'll be burned to a frazzle.'

'Have you got a better idea, Pod? Do you want to wait here until they come and pluck your feathers out one by one?'

Pod stood trembling in his cage. He shook his head.

'What have we got to lose, Pod? Isn't it worth a try?'

'Promise you'll be careful then,' said Pod in a very small voice.

'I promise. Now I need something to use as fuel.'

'Sssssstraw,' muttered Pod.

'Good idea! The straw in our cages is perfect for fuel. Use your beak to wrap some of it around the point where your door was sealed, Pod. Great! And get back as far as you can from the door and stop shaking, will you? I have a feeling this is going to work.'

Kerry extracted Simon's box of matches from where she had hidden it in the hem of her jacket. She lit a green match and threw it at the straw on Pod's door. It immediately flared and sent up a bright flame. White sparks burst outwards from the heart of the flame.

'Yeouch!' cried Pod as one of the sparks flew past him.

'Don't worry! Those sparks are harmless in this dungeon. The dampness will put them out.'

She focused her attention on the fire. The flame grew whiter and the iron bar turned yellow. Then it glowed in a deep shade of orange. Gradually the metal began to melt. Then with a crack and a snap the door sprang open. It swung back and forth on its hinges. Kerry threw her bowl of uneaten turnip and brussels sprout soup straight at the fire and quenched it.

With a heaving and swishing of feathers, Pod flew up out of his cage.

'Well you can still fly,' said Kerry.

'Only barely … It's hard work with this heavy coat of feathers. But now we've got to get you out, Kerry! Can you do the match trick again?'

Kerry found another green match and the same trick worked perfectly the second time. She crawled out of her cage, delighted with her work.

'Isn't it great to be free?' she said.

'Yes, but we're not exactly free yet. How do we get out the dungeon door?'

'That's easy. Get your back to that wall.'

Kerry used the remaining straw and a third green match to set fire to the door. Then she ran to the opposite wall. They stood together with their backs against the wall until the entire door burned down. Finally the flames died out.

'We'd better get out of here,' said Pod, 'before anyone notices we're missing.'

After exiting their little cell, they hurried down a long rocky passage and through the dungeons. They arrived at a junction.

'Can you remember the way out?' Kerry asked.

'It doesn't matter which way we go as long as we get away from those cages,' said Pod zooming on down the wider passage.

Kerry followed Pod as he flew blindly from passage to passage. She hadn't the slightest clue where they were going.

Each route looked exactly the same as the next. Finally they came to a dungeon. To their amazement, before them stood a burned-down door and two cages, just like the ones they had left behind.

'Oh no,' cried Kerry. 'We're back where we started. Look at those brussels sprouts scattered all over the floor. It's the same dungeon we started out from. We've wasted ages running around here like two headless chickens. Are we ever going to stop going around in circles? If we don't get out of here soon, the eagles will discover us missing. It'll soon be morning and they'll be arriving to pluck your feathers.'

'We must be in a maze,' said Pod who was beginning to tremble again. 'We're done for. It's impossible to get out of a maze.'

'My father took us to a maze once when we were little,' said Kerry. 'That was before he went on his fateful voyage and got lost in the Southern Seas.'

'Your father was a very wise man. I'm sure he had no problem getting out of the maze. Which one did he take you to?'

'It was in the Swishtree Forest. And he did show us how to get out of it. Let me see. I wish I could remember.'

'Close your eyes and try to picture it,' said Pod. 'It might come back to you.'

'Yes. Yes, I have it now,' said Kerry. 'You have to make a mark beside every exit you take. That way you can see from the marks if you've been through that exit before.'

'That makes sense,' said Pod. 'Good job you remembered. We could have been wandering around here for years.'

'But what will we use as a marker? In the forest we used chalk.'

'We can use a bit of rock to scrape an X on the wall.'

'Good thinking, Pod.' Kerry picked up a sharp stone and made a rough scrape on the right-hand passage.

'It's only a faint mark but the important thing is that we can see it. And nobody will know how we got out of here. Hopefully when they come looking for us they'll think we're lost in the maze.'

The two friends decided to take all the right turns first and at each junction they marked the wall beside the turn with an X. They kept going until they arrived at a junction, which had already been marked with their X. Here they took the opposite turn. This led them off in a new direction. They kept going, marking every turn they took carefully until finally they found a passage which was much narrower than any they had seen before.

'This is a different type of tunnel. We could be out of the maze,' said Kerry. 'But I suppose we'd better keep marking the walls in case we double back on our tracks again.'

'Let's try to stick to the narrow passages,' said Pod. 'The eagles can't fly here. There's no room for them to stretch their wings.'

They continued on until they heard the sound of rushing water. Following the sound, they travelled along a series of passages. It grew louder and louder. The last passage opened into a huge cavern with a fast-moving river flowing through it. Kerry noticed a little pathway on a ledge to her right. It ran just above the level of the river. And it was going in the direction of the current.

'If we follow this path along with the current it will take us to the sea,' Kerry said, 'and Grinwick told me that the islanders live near the sea caves. We might be able to find them and get help. But we have to move fast. Before long Red Beak will discover us missing and send a search party after us.'

❊❊❊

Simon closed his eyes as he was flung over the edge of the waterfall. The force of the breeze as he fell from the precipice whipped his face. He plummeted downwards towards a swirling torrent below. He hit the water with a slap. Simon held his breath as the falling streams forced him deep into the pool. He fought to free himself from the weight of the falling water, which pushed him down. Then he saw a wooden plank come hurtling towards him. He lunged towards it and grabbed it tightly. He recognised the plank as being a part of the little boat that had fallen apart. Clinging to the plank, Simon floated up to the surface of a fast-flowing river, gasping for air. Gradually his lungs were filled with air and his breathing steadied.

He was being carried in the current of a deep river that rushed away from the high, stone walls of the Abbey, which loomed in the distance behind him. As he looked back at the waterfall he was amazed at the size of its drop. It burst out of a high cliff and fell down into a river below. He knew there was no way out of the current; it was still moving too fast.

Simon was dragged downhill by the rapidly-flowing river.

He clung tightly to his plank of wood, observing the landscape around him. The river was flowing down into a boggy valley. The earth was almost black. Grass grew in tufts along the river-bank. A few trees and bushes were scattered throughout the bog. Simon saw wild birds flying above him, heading for clumps of tall grasses along the banks. In the distance he could see a lake and, beyond, a high mountain range with a central high peak. After what felt like miles the current weakened and Simon could see the mountains more clearly. They were sheer and grey, bleak and rocky and rose to a jagged, purple peak.

Clinging to the plank, he drifted into a lake at the foot of the mountains. He felt chilled to the bone. The strength in his limbs was waning so much that he could barely keep hold of the plank. His hands had grown blue and numb with the cold. As he floated towards the shore he noticed some figures stand-ing at its edge waving at him. He was so frozen that there was no feeling at all left in his limbs. He was shivering violently by the time he got to shore. People at the edge waded into the lake to pull him out. They carried him to a low cliff at the lake edge and entered it through a crack. Inside was a cave, where a fire was burning in a hearth. His wet clothes were peeled off and he was laid on a rough bed by the fire, wrapped in warm blankets.

Simon tried to tell the cave people about Kerry and Pod but his lips were so cold he was unable to speak. One of them lifted his head and offered him a hot drink. It warmed him up slightly but he was shivering so badly that it was difficult to form words.

'Help … my friends …'

'Hey!' He's trying to say something,' said one of the cave people. A few more heads appeared around Simon. Then a woman's voice told him to rest until he was strong enough to speak. They left him alone.

After they had gone, Simon looked around. He noticed that the cave was in fact a living room, with bits of furniture scattered around it. Overwhelmed with exhaustion, he sank back on his rough bed by the fire.

❁❁❁

Simon awoke to see sunlight streaming in through a tiny window that was carved into the cave wall. His eyes were dazzled for a moment and then they focused on a girl with dark brown eyes.

'Am I dreaming?' asked Simon.

'No,' said the girl. 'How do you feel?'

'I'm a bit tired still. I thought I was going to drown back there in a waterfall.'

'You look a bit scratched and bruised but apart from that you're in good shape for someone who survived a fall from the cliff.'

'How long was I asleep?'

'All night,' said the girl.

'And who are you?' Simon asked.

'My name is Niamh. And if you're well enough to get up Simon we'd like to talk to you.'

'How do you know my name?' asked Simon in amazement.

'We've been waiting for you.'

'Do you know about my sister Kerry and Pod, the Blue Owl.'

'I know that Red Beak has them up in the Abbey.'

'He caught Kerry then?'

'Hurry up and get dressed,' said Niamh. 'There's someone here who wants to meet you. He will tell you all the news.'

CHAPTER 12

The Library

Kerry and Pod followed the underground river, hoping to see a glimmer of daylight around every bend. The caves on each bank grew smaller and stretched off in different directions. They arrived at a domed cave and to their surprise discovered some ornate wooden chairs and tables stored in its recesses. The next cave was filled with old church pews. An adjoining one contained crates of candles and old tablecloths. And adjacent to that was a cave full of ancient books.

'Look at this, Kerry,' said Pod, landing on one of the crates and studying its contents. 'It's a book on science and nature. And see the next book is all about the history of the Abbey. But the amazing thing is that they have been handwritten and illustrated.'

'They're manuscripts,' said Kerry. 'See the beautiful drawings on the side of this one. The monks must have spent years working on those.'

'Do you know, I think these books belong to a library? All of them are indexed under various categories. Take a look at the first page of this one.'

'You're right,' said Kerry wearily. 'But that means that we must be still underneath the Abbey. We're still walking around in circles. I can't believe it.'

'There must be a library above us,' said Pod. 'See over there, that looks like a door up high in the wall.'

Pod flew up to inspect the door. Kerry found some roughly hewn steps and followed him to the door. She pushed it open. They could see a flight of stairs beyond. They climbed it. A small door stood at the top with a tiny sliver of light glowing under it.

'Follow the light,' said Pod.

Kerry pushed the door and it opened easily into a circular room. Silently, they entered and looked around. The walls were lined with rows and rows of books in heavy mahogany cases. In the centre of the room, an enormous spiral staircase led up to the next floor. A circle of desks were placed around the foot of the staircase. Each one had a reading lamp attached. There were no windows but a huge shaft of light flooded the staircase.

'We are still underground,' said Kerry. 'All that sunlight means that the next floor has to be at ground level.'

'This may well have been the room where the monks worked on their manuscripts,' said Pod. 'See, the desks all have inkwells and bookstands. These reading lamps are perfect for such detailed work.'

'Look over here,' said Kerry. 'Somebody has been working here quite recently. This manuscript is open and the inkwell is full of ink.'

They studied the manuscript. The page lying open contained a passage from the ancient Book of Isaiah. It was unfinished. Pod started to read the last lines that had been written.

> forget the former things;
> do not dwell in the past.
> See I am doing a new thing!
> Now it springs up; do you not perceive it?
> I am making a way in the desert
> And streams in the wasteland.
> The wild animals honour me,
> the jackals and the owls,
> because I provide water in the desert.

The remaining pages were blank.

'I think there are monks still working here,' said Pod. 'This is definitely a work still in progress. Eagles can't write like this. Maybe if we found the monks, they would help us to escape.'

'No, Pod,' said Kerry. 'We must get out of here.'

'And keep going around in circles down in the dungeons,' Pod's voice echoed from the spiral staircase above her.

'Come back, Pod,' called Kerry. But he was gone. Reluctantly, she followed him.

Kerry mounted the spiral staircase to a high-ceilinged room on the next floor. It was filled with light and Pod was flitting from window to window. This room was also circular in shape and contained no books at all. Seven pointed windows stood in a semicircle overlooking a series of beautiful gardens. In the sunlight they saw two cascading fountains flanking a long white-pebbled driveway. Flower gardens adjoined the main lawn and beyond these Kerry saw a shrubbery and small grove leading up to the high walls of the Abbey. All this she could see from the seven windows. At each end of the semicircle stood an archway leading to further rooms. Three larger windows dominated the other half of the circular room. They overlooked the Abbey's cloisters which formed a corridor of slender arches around a square garden. A tall stone tower stood at the opposite end of the square.

The spiral staircase continued up to further floors. Entranced by the beauty of the light-filled rooms, Pod flew on upwards and Kerry followed. She realised the vastness of the library when she reached the next floor. The central room at the top of the stairs was again circular in shape but much smaller than the room underneath. This room, which was also lined with manuscripts, had two arched openings at either end. Each archway led to another room, which in turn led to further rooms.

'This floor holds books that are all about birds and animals of the woodlands,' said Pod. 'Each level must have a different theme.'

He had flown up to the next storey before Kerry could stop him. She followed him again and found him looking at a table full of open books on cookery and medicinal remedies. They were filled with beautiful drawings and diagrams. In an adjoining room was a mahogany desk with several chairs placed around it. A book was left open on a table. Kerry ran over and picked it up. The open page contained a recipe for growing owl's feathers.

'This is where they got your feather-growing formula,' Kerry said. She looked at the title of the book.

'Ancient Remedies and Potions,' she read and began to flick through it.

'Look, Pod, there's a recipe here for laughing gas; wouldn't it be fun to try it on Red Beak? It says here that it makes people laugh so hard that they have to bend over to hold their tummies. Then they fall down laughing and roll around the floor in helpless fits of hysteria. They end up with a terrible fit of sneezing. There's a warning here that says if you take too much of the potion you could die of laughter. The effects are also very contagious and can last for hours.'

She started to read out the ingredients:

Half a cup of fine ash from a fireplace

2 teaspoons of strong white pepper

A large bottle of the fizziest orange

Two cups of finely chopped red onions

7 teaspoons of pollen taken from large red tulips

4 whisked egg whites

And 10 liquorice sweets mashed into a pulp

Method: Place all the ingredients together in a large saucepan and set on a fire. Boil until the mixture turns red with blue bubbles. Then wait for white smoke to appear …

Pod had happened upon another book and was studying it intently.

'Kerry this one is called *The History of the Abbey of Dun Ruah* and it's got a map of all the secret underground passages on the island. Look, this is the layout of the Abbey and there's an underground passage here that leads all the way to the main village. This is our chance to escape. Let me work it out. Where exactly are we now?'

Pod was interrupted from his reading by the sounds of eagles' wings flapping in the distance.

'We'd better get out of here,' he whispered.

They headed down the staircase until they reached the ground floor. Pod flew to a window.

'Let's make for the grove outside,' he said.

Kerry had just reached the window and had managed to push the sash up when she heard a menacing cry behind them.

'What's going on here?'

They spun around to see Roddick, the chief guard, perched on top of the spiral staircase.

'Follow me, Kerry!' cried Pod as he flew through the window.

Kerry clambered over the windowsill and jumped to the lawn below. She chased after Pod, who was already halfway to the Abbey wall. An eagle swooped towards her with its massive claws outstretched. She avoided it by inches. By now Pod had reached the Abbey wall. Kerry was close behind him, when the second eagle came at her from behind. It grabbed her by the shoulders, lifting her high into the air. Kerry struggled to free herself, but a third eagle had arrived on the scene. It pounced on her legs and between them the two giant birds carried her back through the library window. Within seconds another eagle followed with Pod in his clutches. They were dropped on the library floor before Roddick.

'Did you think you could get away from us that easily?' Roddick hissed. 'This is a large palace but we also have a great number of well-trained guards on patrol. There is no escaping the great King of the Eagles.'

He turned to his henchmen.

'King Red Beak has found a safer place to keep the poor, neurotic Blue Owl and his brave friend, Miss Macken. This time they will be placed in the prison tower with a 24-hour guard. How sad they look now that their escape attempt didn't work. But at least they got a little tour of the Abbey and the exercise will have done them good. Guards, take them away and chain them to their cages. I'll send the Palace Plucker down immediately to remove the owl's feathers. And I'll tell him to show no mercy.'

Roddick flew off.

Kerry and Pod were seized by two strong eagles and carried through the arched doorway and into a great library hall. They were taken to a side door and pushed through. The eagles escorted them across the ancient cloisters to the tall round tower which they said was the palace prison. Here they threw Kerry and Pod behind bars and handcuffed them in chains.

'His Majesty's bodyguards will be standing on guard outside the tower,' explained one of the eagles. 'We've been ordered to keep watch here day and night so there's no point in trying to escape again. Now let me do a body search on you both.'

Kerry was held by one of the eagles while another searched her clothes.

'What do we have here?' said the guard as he pulled the matchbox out of Kerry's pocket.

'This must be what you used to melt the seals on your cages and burn the dungeon door down. I'm sure the King and Queen will find this piece of evidence very interesting!'

Taking the matches with them, the two eagles departed.

Kerry and Pod sat waiting in terror for the Palace Plucker. To their horror he arrived within minutes. Two eagle guards escorted him into the cell. He was a mean-looking creature with a long, hooked beak. A giant tweezers protruded from either side of the beak. This he removed with his right claw and held it up in the air, examining it closely. One of the guards hung a wooden perch from the ceiling in the middle of the prison cell and forced Pod to stand on it. Then the Palace Plucker tested out the tweezers on some weeds that were growing through a crack in the floor.

'A bit rusty I think. Let me polish it up a little.'

Pod broke into a fit of hiccups as the Palace Plucker produced a huge duster from under his wing and started to polish the tweezers vigorously. Soon it was gleaming.

'That's better,' he said, holding the glittering instrument up to the light and studying it from tip to tip. He hopped over to Pod on one claw, with the tweezers held in the other. Pod was struggling with the chain that held him to the bars of the cell.

His wings flapped furiously in a desperate attempt to break free.

'Control yourself,' cried the plucker, 'or I'll have to call for help.' He lunged at Pod, brandishing the tweezers.

CHAPTER 13

Browdan

Simon looked around the little whitewashed cave room in which he had spent the night. A small fire was burning in the grate and a tiny window gave enough light for him to find his clothes. They lay in a neat pile on a wooden chest beside the bed. He realised that the lake people had washed and dried his clothes from the night before. When he stood to dress he saw that his body was covered in bruises. But despite some tenderness he felt well rested. He dressed and opened a low door into a pretty kitchen with a big open fire burning in the hearth. Two old, wooden dressers leaned against the white walls. The room was lit by one tiny window low down in the uneven wall of the cave dwelling.

Niamh was preparing breakfast.

'Sit down at the table,' she said, 'and help yourself. You must be starving.'

Simon sat down at a long wooden table, which was laid with

fresh bread and toast. Niamh set plates of boiled eggs and pancakes before him. The sight of the food made his mouth water and he tucked into a hearty breakfast.

The sound of footsteps approaching caused Simon to look up.

'He's here!' exclaimed Niamh as she hurried to open the door.

A tall man with dark hair entered the room. A Tawny Owl was perched on one of his shoulders and on the other was a sparrow. Three other birds followed: a hawk, a blackbird and a thrush. They perched on top of one of the dressers watching the man intently. Despite his ragged, threadbare clothes and his lean, rugged appearance, Simon could see he was a dignified and noble man.

'This is my brother Browdan,' said Niamh. 'He is the leader of all the cave dwellers on the island.'

Simon stood up to shake his hand. Browdan had a wise face. His brown, twinkling eyes and gentle smile made Simon feel comfortable with him straight away.

'It's great to meet you Browdan and thanks for looking after me last night.'

'I had no hand in that Simon. I don't live on this part of the island. I live in the sea caves. But I got word from my sister and from Cian, the leader of the lake people, that you were here. They sent me a message through the freebirds of the island that you needed help. So I came here as fast as I could.'

'They are beautiful birds,' said Simon admiring the Tawny Owl who reminded him so much of Pod.

'Without their help, Simon, the cave settlements wouldn't have survived this long. The birds of the lakes and forests let us know whenever Red Beak sends his guards out to plunder the island. They also act as messengers between the many cave settlements on the island, keeping us in touch with one another.'

'Do many people live in the caves?' Simon asked.

'There are about two hundred living around this lake altogether. But throughout the island there are thousands living in caves. At one time there were four main villages on the island,' said Browdan. 'Coracle was the largest one and it was there that the Chieftain lived. His name was Coleman Cooley and he was our father. All the villages are deserted now since Red Beak attacked us.'

'So you are the children of Coleman Cooley,' said Simon. 'I thought his whole family were murdered by Red Beak.'

'Our parents were killed by Red Beak himself,' said Niamh. 'He also killed my twin brother, Coleman, who was a monk. But we still live here in the island's caves and we believe that someday soon the Eagle King will fall from power.'

'I like this cave,' said Simon. 'It's very comfortable and it's peaceful. I slept like a log.'

'Yes, some of the outer caves here are natural. More of them were dug out of the cliffs around the lake by our people,' said Niamh, 'but most of the island population lives in the sea caves. They are much larger.'

'And are you safe here from the eagles?'

'In the early days, when we first moved into the caves,' said

Browdan, 'the eagles patrolled the island on a daily basis. That was after Red Beak threw us out of our homes. We often went back to the villages to collect furniture and possessions from our houses. Whenever we did, the eagles would attack us. They killed and mutilated many of our families and friends.'

'So they behave like terrorists,' said Simon.

'Yes. Red Beak has used his philosophy of "Eagle Power" to brainwash his flocks. They are trained to destroy using military strategies and tactics. They approach silently, ambushing their victims from behind. Then they sink their sharp claws into the neck and peck at the shoulders. Hundreds of the villagers were killed and maimed by the eagles. So we had to stop going out by day. Now we only venture out at night-time under the cover of darkness. And we have developed some strategies of our own to deal with the eagles.'

'I would never live under Red Beak's reign of terror,' said Simon.

'But we love our families and this is our ancestral home. If we left the island we would lose all our history and traditions,' said Browdan. 'We are not ready to give up.'

'But Red Beak is making your lives a misery.'

'It's not so bad,' said Niamh. 'Our homes are very comfortable, and a lot of these caves are linked together by tunnels. So we can meet together without having to go out of doors. There are very few entrances to the caves so it's easy to guard them. If the eagles come spying around here we can protect ourselves very easily. They've no idea how many of us are living on the island. Red Beak thinks that most of the population left the island with the monks five years ago. So now they don't come around here so often. We are left pretty much on our own.'

'But what do you live on?'

'It's tough trying to eke out an existence here, Simon,' said Browdan. 'We live off the fish from the lake and the sea and eggs from birds that nest in the boglands. We plant some crops wherever we can, like potatoes and root vegetables. We have to be very careful because if the eagles find them, they destroy our crops. Of course, we live in hope that someday we'll reclaim our homes. But I didn't come here to tell you all our problems. I came to give you news of your two friends, Kerry and Pod.'

'You've got news?'

'Yes. They are being held as prisoners by Red Beak up in the Abbey. We know exactly where they are.'

'Oh no, they've caught Kerry as well!' exclaimed Simon.

'They are both being held in the dungeons. But Niamh thinks it will be possible to rescue them down there.'

'Really?'

'Yes. It's a bit risky but when you are ready Niamh will take you there through the underground passages. She knows the Abbey like the back of her hand. But maybe you need to rest a bit more. The lake people were very worried about you last night. You were exhausted after your ordeal and frozen stiff. They're amazed you didn't get hypothermia.'

'I'm made of tough stuff,' Simon laughed. 'But tell me this; where did you get all this information about Kerry and Pod and how did you know my name?'

'The Messenger told us. He sent word.'

'The Messenger!' exclaimed Simon.

'Yes,' said Browdan, 'do you know him?'

'No, I've never met him but Grinwick, the eagle who brought us here, told us about him. He said he comes from an ancient realm that goes back as far as the dawn of time. He also said that many people don't believe in him.'

'The Messenger is as real as you or me,' Browdan said, 'and he is well known by the islanders here. At present he is working with the Abbot of the Ark of Dun Ruah. He has always guarded and protected us during hard times. He is a powerful prophet and has promised that one day soon he will help us defeat the Eagle King. I believe that his prophecy is about to be fulfilled.'

'Is he here on the island?'

'We haven't seen him here yet. But I'm convinced that he has been on the island lately. I sense his presence near us. He is a master of silence. He can come and go without being seen or heard. That way he can make his own assessment of the situation.'

'Like a spy,' Simon added.

Browdan laughed. 'When the Messenger chooses to appear among us we will be ready to do his bidding.'

'What about my sister Kerry and Pod the owl? Do you really think that Niamh and I can get into the dungeons and rescue them?'

'It's worth a try. There are many good eagles working in the Abbey. They are forced into slavery under Red Beak but remain friends to us cave dwellers. We have sent word to them about you through the freebirds. When the time comes they will help you. But now Niamh has volunteered to go back to the dungeons with you. She has a detailed knowledge of the cave system under the Abbey. And she will take you straight to their cell.'

'I'm ready to go whenever you are, Niamh,' said Simon.

'Then I'll go and prepare for the journey,' said Niamh.

During the morning Browdan introduced Simon to Cian, the leader of the lake clan. Cian was a young, fair-haired man, strong and friendly with intelligent eyes. He took Simon on a tour of the caves, showing him the homes of the lake people, their schoolrooms and workplaces. Simon saw how the network of cave dwellings were linked together by passages and tunnels. Cian also provided him with food and some camouflage for the journey.

Before they set out for the Abbey, Browdan took Simon aside. 'When you find Kerry and Pod, get out of the Abbey as fast as you can. Niamh will lead you to the sea caves near the village of Coracle. She will bring you to our hidden town by the underground lake. From there we will get you off the island. Also, I have confirmed that the freebirds of the island have sent word to the good eagles in the Abbey, to tell them you're on your way. They will be watching out for you. Many of the eagles inside the Abbey are tired of Red Beak and his tyranny, but are too frightened to leave him. They are willing to help you. You will not be alone in there. So take heart and be courageous.'

CHAPTER 14

Niamh

Simon thanked Browdan, Cian and the lake people for saving his life and giving him shelter. It was still early when he set out on his journey back to the Abbey with Niamh. He followed her along the riverbank back to the waterfall where he had fallen the previous day. The lake people had given them broad-brimmed hats covered with twigs and leaves for camouflage. Wearing these they stayed close to trees and large scrub so they could take shelter if they sighted marauding eagles.

Soon they reached the waterfall. Simon stood for a moment watching the majestic sight of the river bursting from the cliff face and plummeting into the lake below.

'How did I survive that?' he gasped.

'You must have nine lives,' said Niamh.

She beckoned for him to follow her and showed him how to climb the rocky precipice at the side of the falls. Sticking their feet and hands into little crevices in the cliff face, they climbed closer and closer to the mouth of the waterfall. The roar of the plummeting water was deafening and the rock was so slippy that Simon feared he would lose his grip. At last Niamh stopped at a wide crack in the rock. Here she entered the cliff face. Simon followed her inside to a low and narrow passage. They crawled on hands and knees for a while but soon it widened and rose in height making it possible to walk upright. Simon saw that Niamh was an expert at finding her way through the underground caves. She told him how as a young girl she had discovered the layout of the Abbey while playing with her twin brother, Coleman.

'The whole Abbey is riddled with underground passages linking one part to another,' she said. 'Coleman and I played up around the Abbey all the time when we were little. We were fascinated by the high walls and ancient buildings. And the monks were very kind to us. They didn't seem to mind us snooping around. One day we stumbled upon a secret passage leading into the Abbey. Coleman literally fell into a hole in the forest floor outside the Abbey walls. Later we discovered that the hole was an entrance to a network of tunnels that spread under the entire island. We kept coming back here and found more and more passages every day. We discovered that many of them led to the ancient Abbey library. Coleman and I would often creep in there when the monks left for vespers. We discovered that the library was filled with priceless manuscripts. And our father told us that monks came here throughout the ages from all over the world to study the art of manuscript illumination. They say the library has the largest collection of original manuscripts in the world.'

'I've never heard of it,' said Simon.

'Oh the monks didn't publicise this fact. The existence of the library was a well-kept secret among scholars. We loved to look at the beautiful hand-drawn pictures in the books. They weren't all spiritual books either. There were books on all sorts of subjects. Coleman fell in love with the place. He began to borrow books and copy them at home at night-time. By the time he joined the order when he was thirteen he was the best illuminator in the Abbey; probably the best they ever had.'

'I take it that an illuminator is an illustrator,' said Simon.

'Yes, the illuminators are artists and experts in calligraphy. They draw pictures to illustrate the script they are writing and they decorate the script with beautiful colours.'

By now Niamh and Simon had entered a maze. Simon was impressed at the way Niamh picked her way through the complex layout of passages and caves. As they zigzagged their way through an intricate mesh of intersections and forked junctions Niamh never hesitated over which path to choose. She seemed to know exactly where she was going. Before long they had arrived at the dungeons. They made their way through a corridor of empty cells until Niamh stopped at a burned-out door. Two empty cages were all that remained inside.

'They're gone,' said Niamh.

Simon looked around the cell for some sign of what had happened.

'Look at this,' he said, 'it's one of my matches. And here's another one. Good for Kerry. She must have used them to burn the locks off the cages. And then she burned down the door. Clever girl! They managed to escape.'

'But where did they go from here?' said Niamh.

They searched around the dungeons looking for clues and footprints but the ground was paved with hard stone and they couldn't tell which direction Kerry and Pod had taken.

'We'd better get out of here,' said Niamh. 'Red Beak may not have discovered that they are missing yet. The eagles could return here at any moment and they'll be angry to find this mess. Red Beak will raid the whole island when he finds his prisoners missing. We could all be in great danger.'

They hurried down the corridor that led out of the dungeons. Niamh paused to examine the markings on the junction walls. She pointed to an X scratched out on a tunnel entrance.

'These are fresh markings,' she said. 'Kerry and Pod made these while they were trying to get out of here. They must have been going around in circles for quite a while. I don't think they are too far ahead of us. If we're lucky we might catch up with them.'

As they followed the passages, the ground became soft and earthy, and Kerry's footprints appeared from time to time. From these details Niamh was able to tell the way they had gone. Their tracks led them to the underground river. Here Niamh stopped to study the ground.

'I can see Kerry's footprints all over this path. It runs along the river edge all the way back to the Abbey. I know the river path well. It goes under the library to the kitchen cellars.

They've headed straight into danger.'

'We've no choice but to follow them,' said Simon.

'But we could be killed.'

'There's got to be a way to find them without the eagles catching us. Think about it, Niamh. You know all the secret passages.'

'Well, there was a tiny, secret passage leading from the kitchen cellars to Red Beak's Great Hall. It was built inside the walls themselves and runs through the main rooms in the Abbey. It was very old and crumbling when I was a child and it may have fallen in by now. But it might be worth trying to find it. It would be a very safe place to hide out, that's if we managed to get in there. I've heard that Red Beak holds most of his conferences in the Great Hall with his guards.'

'It sounds like the perfect place for us to spy for information,' said Simon. 'We could eavesdrop on one of his conferences and find out what his plans are.'

'But going back to the Abbey is very risky,' warned Niamh. 'We could both be caught. I don't want to do it.'

'Oh come on, Niamh! It's time you people plucked up some courage and took a few risks,' said Simon. 'Why don't you stand up to that eagle beast?'

'You don't know what Red Beak is capable of. You haven't seen him in action like we islanders have.'

'Look, Niamh, I know you've gone through a rough time with those eagles. But what was the point in coming all this way for nothing, can you tell me that?'

'I'm scared Simon. Red Beak's guards have widened the

passages under the Abbey. So they can fly around most of them. And I've heard they've blocked up the smaller tunnels that they don't use. The place is crawling with guards and it would be almost impossible to escape them. We'd be heading straight into their lair!'

'We're all scared, Niamh, but we've got to think of the others. You've led me into the dungeons and through the maze to here. It's obvious that Red Beak hasn't blocked up all the passages. If he had we wouldn't have got through. You know the Abbey like the back of your hand and your instincts are spot on. You've taught me how to free climb a cliff face and I've seen the way you followed Kerry's tracks. If anyone can find Kerry and Pod, you can! Please, Niamh. Their lives are at stake and I can't make it in there without you.'

Niamh sighed and twisted her long black hair into a knot. 'Maybe you're right, Simon. Maybe it's time I faced my fears and took a risk. OK, I'll take you to the secret passage if you promise that you will do exactly what I say.'

'It's a deal,' said Simon.

Niamh led Simon along the river caves to the cellars under the library. The ground became stoney and they lost sight of Kerry's footprints. They continued on to the cellars underneath the kitchens. Niamh made her way into a small cellar and rummaged around behind some old wine casks until she found what she was looking for.

'Here's the entrance to the secret passage that passes through the walls of the Abbey,' she said.

Niamh pulled a loose stone out of the way and slipped into

the passage. Simon followed and pulled the stone back into place behind him. To their relief, the way was clear. It was narrow and cramped and as they progressed they found that it had fallen in at several places. But they managed to clear the rubble from the steps and passages and make it all the way to the fireplace in the Great Hall. They sat deep in the shadows of the fireplace, hidden by the black, sooty mantle. Time moved slowly as they waited for the eagles to appear. Simon scratched his head impatiently.

'Where are they?' he moaned.

'Be still,' whispered Niamh. 'I hear someone coming across the main courtyard.'

CHAPTER 15

Fireworks

In the prison tower the Palace Plucker polished his big, shiny tweezers. With great care he held them up to the light and inspected them. Then he fixed his red eyes on Pod. His gaze was icy as he approached the shivering owl. Just as he lunged at him the door was flung open. Roddick, the chief guard, flew into the room followed by six of his henchmen.

'Get off him,' he yelled.

'But I've been ordered to pluck him,' cried the Palace Plucker.

'Out of my way,' ordered Roddick. 'Queen Kiki wants to see the prisoners. Guards, unlock the cages.'

One of the guards brushed past the Palace Plucker and opened the cage doors. Kerry and Pod were led from the prison tower out to the cloisters. They were escorted past the library, through an arched gateway and into the main courtyard at the front of the Abbey. The guards led the prisoners across the courtyard to the doors of the Great Hall. They entered and were ordered to wait before the two golden thrones for the arrival of the Queen.

Within minutes a dozen eagle bodyguards arrived through the main doors of the Abbey followed by the Queen's entourage. A golden bugle was sounded to announce her arrival. Queen Kiki came through the doors, perched on a bright red carpet, the edges of which were held in the beaks of eight eagle porters. They laid the carpet in front of her throne. Queen Kiki wore a tiara of glittering diamonds topped with a headdress of long scarlet feathers. She was draped in a cloak of red and white plumes with a flush of royal blue. She glided off the carpet, hopped up onto her throne perch and looked down at her minions.

'Who are these?' she asked a tall eagle who looked like her chief bodyguard. He promptly whispered something into her ear.

'Oh yes. How forgetful of me! It's the Blue Owl. Very nice feathers! They'll do beautifully. So don't try escaping again. We need those feathers. It's your patriotic duty to stay here and provide me with feathers for the rest of your life.'

'But how could it be my patriotic duty?' said Pod. 'I'm not a resident of Eyrie Island.'

'Don't interrupt. And you! Young lady,' she said turning to Kerry, 'I want to talk to you about those matches. Guards, bring me the matches. Oh, here they are. Hand me my spectacles.'

The bodyguard handed the Queen a large pair of round

spectacles studded with diamonds. She perched them on her beak and started to read from the matchbox.

'HANDY MATCHES ... FOR ALL YOUR RECREATIONAL NEEDS: HOUSE FIRES, TORCHES, DAZZLING FIREWORKS, BONFIRES, BARBECUES AND MUCH MORE ...'

'Can you tell me, my dear girl, do these matches really make fireworks? I simply love fireworks of all kinds. Back home on the Island of Iolathar we had fireworks for every occasion and it was such fun. But this island is so dull. I get so bored. Do entertain me.'

'My brother invented them,' replied Kerry.

'Well, demonstrate, my girl, before I lose my patience. But don't damage anything, for heaven's sake. I don't want my beautiful palace going on fire.'

'It's an abbey,' corrected Pod.

'Stop interrupting, you rude owl.'

'Those are not my matches,' said Kerry, 'and I don't know how to make fireworks.'

'Nonsense, I order you to demonstrate now. If you don't do what I say I will lock you in the tower and leave you in solitary confinement, without food and water for a week.'

Kerry slowly stepped up to the throne, took the box of matches and opened it. There were only two matches left in the box, one white and one red. All the green matches were gone. Kerry racked her brain. She knew the white matches were for light but what did the red stand for?

'These white matches are torches,' said Kerry, lighting it for

Queen Kiki and holding it before her.

'That's not very interesting,' said the Queen. 'Light a different one.'

'The last match is red,' said Kerry. 'If you give me a piece of wood from the fireplace over there I'll see what I can do.'

One of the guards handed Kerry a log from the grate. She held it in her right hand and studied it for a few moments, her mind working on all possibilities. Then she lit the match and set fire to the log. The log lit up in an instant and burned like a torch with a bright yellow flame. Kerry threw the log high into the air above the eagles' heads, hoping to frighten them away. As it soared towards the ceiling the flames changed from yellow to green. With a mighty crack the log exploded and the eagles shrieked. A torrent of pink sparks burst from the log's core. They cascaded slowly down into the room like a sparkling pink waterfall. The glittering sparks landed in a pool on the floor and with a flicker they were suddenly gone.

'Wonderful,' cried Queen Kiki, jumping up from her throne with excitement. Her surprised entourage immediately joined her in cheering the display.

'More,' she cried. 'Show me more!'

Suddenly, to everyone's surprise, including Kerry's, the sparks flared up again swirling like a tornado in the centre of the room. They shot high up into the air and converged in the shape of a dazzling star, which spun and twirled across the ceiling. It circled around the flocks of fascinated eagles. Then it burst into a sizzling ball of fire, spraying showers of multicoloured beams outwards in fountains of light. They faded and reformed into a multicoloured rainbow, which extended as an arch over the entire length of the room. It shimmered and glowed for several minutes. Gradually, it faded away.

'Marvellous!' Queen Kiki again rose from her throne in delight and flapped her wings. 'That was absolutely wonderful. Do another trick for me now, I command you!'

'But I have no matches left – they're all gone!'

'Well get them!'

'But I can't get them.'

Queen Kiki screamed and stamped her claws in rage.

'Where did you buy them? I'll send my eagles to get them. You must tell them where to go.'

'But they're not on sale. They are my brother Simon's invention. Only he knows what ingredients go into those matches.'

'And where is Simon?' demanded Kiki.

Kerry shrugged her shoulders.

'I want those ingredients,' cried Kiki who was almost dancing with rage. 'Guards, make her tell me where Simon is.'

An idea suddenly flashed into Kerry's head. She thought of the laughing gas recipe she had seen in the great library with Pod. She strained to remember the list of ingredients. Just as the eagles rushed towards her she found herself raising her hand.

'Stop,' she said. 'Maybe I can remember Simon's ingredients. Wait. Let me think … Half a cup of fine ash from a fireplace … Two teaspoons of strong white pepper …'

'Write this down,' Kiki ordered her guards.

When Kerry got to the end of the list she added two extra

items – a pair of gas masks.

'What do you want the gas masks for?' asked Queen Kiki.

'Making Handy Matches is a dangerous procedure,' said Kerry. 'My brother always wears a gas mask. And now for the method. What a pity I can't remember how Simon made them. I will have to start from scratch and experiment. I'm sure it will all come back to me if you give me a stove to work on and a large saucepan.'

'Just tell my guards what you need and they will provide you with everything,' said Queen Kiki.

'I also need Pod to help me. He is the only one who knows how to assist me. And he must be in the full of his health. Making matches is hard work and it's easy to make a mistake. Pod must be fit and that means he must have all his feathers. So the Palace Plucker will have to wait until we are finished. It's dangerous working with fire and I need to be able to concentrate without anyone looking over my shoulder.'

'Damn you and your conditions. Who do you think you are making such demands of me the great Queen Kiki? One of my guards will assist you.'

'It won't work. I need someone who is trained in pyrotechnics. Pod is the only one who can do it.'

'Oh very well then,' said Queen Kiki, 'but I demand to see another firework display the minute you are finished. Guards, take them back to the prison tower. Make sure they have everything they need. Start working on it as soon as they bring you the ingredients.'

Queen Kiki rose from her throne fluttering her red and

white plumes. She mounted her travelling carpet.

'Footmen,' she called in a shrill voice. Her eight eagle porters took their places around the carpet catching the edges up in their beaks. Holding the carpet with Queen Kiki balanced on top, they conveyed her down the Great Hall and out through the front door. The cortège of eagles-in-waiting followed her.

CHAPTER 16

A Laughing Matter

Simon and Niamh were still sitting in their hiding place inside the fireplace of the Great Hall. From this great vantage point they witnessed Kerry's impressive fireworks display and her conversation with the Queen. Kerry didn't realise that Simon had helped her with her firework display. After the pink sparkling cascade faded and he heard the Queen shouting for more he decided to join in the fun. He picked out a handful of matches from inside his jacket, lit them and tossed them out into the room. This caused sparks to flare up like a tornado in the centre of the room. The eagles were so focused on the dazzling fireworks, that they didn't see Simon craning his head out of the fireplace. He laughed when he saw the look of surprise on Kerry's face as she watched the amazing firework display work its magic on the Eagle Queen.

When Kerry and Pod left the hall, Simon turned to Niamh.

'We've got to go to the prison tower and get them out of

there. I don't know where Kerry got that crazy list of ingredients. She must be playing for time. But we'll have to go underground. This place is crawling with eagle guards.'

'Yes and not just eagles. I can see a pair of green swiftails too.'

'Green swiftails ... where?'

'They're spying through a peephole in the wall ... up there.'

'They're not spies. That's Timmy and Dot, our friends. They must have followed us here. I've got to catch their attention.'

'The room looks empty,' said Niamh, 'but be careful. There could be eagle spies lurking in the corners.'

Simon lit a purple match. A bright plume of purple gas emerged from it and swirled up to Timmy and Dot's peephole. It exploded into sizzling sparks. Timmy looked out and saw the sparks floating up from the fireplace. Then he saw Simon with his head leaning out, beckoning to them to come down. Delighted and relieved to see him, Timmy and Dot flew straight down from their perch on the wall. They joined Simon and Niamh in the fireplace.

❂❂❂

Kerry and Pod were escorted back across the main courtyard and through the cloisters to the tower. Four guards locked and chained them into their cages. Then they stood outside the prison cell guarding them. Pod turned to Kerry with a puzzled look on his face.

'What was that all about?' he whispered. 'You can't make matches.'

'I'm not making matches, Pod.'

'But what was that list of ingredients all about?'

'Look, I'll explain later when we have some privacy.'

Before long, six eagles arrived at the tower with the ingredients, a pair of gas masks, one large saucepan and a little stove. They released Kerry and Pod from their chains and joined the other guards outside guarding the door.

'What are you doing? Pod persisted. 'When they find out that you're spoofing, we're dead.'

'I'm making laughing gas,' whispered Kerry, 'and I've remembered all the ingredients. Aren't you proud of me?'

Pod looked aghast. His beak hung wide open, his face tilted to one side with his feathers standing on end.

'But you don't know what you're doing. Haven't I told you how dangerous it is messing about with strange recipes and potions?'

'But this is a chance to escape!'

'Have you thought about how it's going to affect us? I once knew a man who took laughing gas and he ended up in an early grave. He actually died of laughter!'

'We'll be fine. All we have to do is put the gas masks on. Then we won't be affected by the laughing gas. I've thought up a great escape plan. When we've made the recipe we'll call the guards back in here. They'll inhale the laughing gas and we will make a run for it. We'll head for the library – it is just across the cloisters. Then we'll get that book you found with all the underground maps and we'll know exactly how to get out of here. This time we'll be ready to make our escape properly.'

'But, Kerry, you've got to listen to me. Laughing gas is extremely dangerous,' said Pod. His eyes began to twitch. 'It's worse than playing with fire. What if it doesn't wear off? I for one don't fancy spending the rest of my days rolling around here laughing like a clown and making a fool out of myself every time I open my mouth.'

'Oh, don't be such an old grump, Pod. Do you want all your feathers plucked out? We don't have many choices here. It's either feather plucking or laughing gas. Choose your poison?'

Pod grumbled under his breath while Kerry took out the ingredients and started to make the concoction.

'Potions can have strange side effects,' said Pod, his large crop of feathers all fluffed out. 'I once knew an owl who used vanishing cream on his beak to make it look smaller. When he looked in the mirror, his entire head was missing. And it never came back. He remained headless for the rest of his life.'

'We have to take the chance, Pod.'

'But I had another friend—'

'Stop arguing and relax. Your feathers are all standing up. You look scarier than the headless owl.'

Despite much more complaining from Pod, they brewed up the mixture together. When it started to bubble Kerry put the lid on the pot to stop the gas escaping. She ordered Pod to put on the gas mask. It was a bit big and she spent some time adjusting the straps to make it fit. She put on her own gas mask and then removed the lid from the pot. Then she banged on the cell door, calling the guards and shouting.

'The matches are ready!'

The six guards rushed in together and saw Kerry and Pod with the gas masks on. Immediately, they started to giggle. And Kerry knew the gas was taking effect.

'Look at the owl with the gas mask on,' they laughed. 'He looks so silly.' They bent over laughing noisily and fell to the floor.

Soon they were laughing so hard that they didn't notice Kerry and Pod slipping out the door. They left the guards guffawing loudly, rolling about on the floor, with tears streaming down their faces. There was such a commotion that Kerry closed the door and locked it behind them to block out the noise.

Outside in the cloistered square they hurried through the long, arched passageway that led straight to the library. Entering it through a small side door, they turned left towards the library hall. They found their way to the circular room with the spiral staircase without much trouble and hurried up the stairs. Then they set about looking for the geography room where they had seen the book of underground maps.

Pod flew ahead of Kerry and found the room first. But he saw that the map was no longer on the table where they had last seen it.

'It's gone,' he said when Kerry entered.

'Somebody must have put it back on the shelves,' said Kerry. 'We've got to search the room. It has to be here somewhere.'

Pod flew up to the highest shelves and Kerry searched the lower rows of the many bookcases that lined the walls of the room. But, try as they might, they couldn't find the book anywhere.

'I told you,' said Pod, 'we shouldn't have made that laughing gas. Now we're in bigger trouble—'

'Shhhh! I hear someone coming.'

They rushed to hide under the table, crouching low beneath it. To their surprise they heard the sound of human footsteps approaching.

Through the archway a man in a grey, hooded cloak appeared. He entered the room. To Kerry's dismay he walked straight up to their table and bent down. He looked right into her eyes.

CHAPTER 17

The Prophet

The man in the grey, hooded cloak studied Kerry with his piercing green eyes.

'Don't be afraid,' he said.

'But who are you?' asked Pod.

'I am the Messenger.'

'Are you the prophet that the wise old owls talk about?' asked Pod, emerging from under the table.

'I'm known as a prophet. But my friends call me Malachy.'

Pod gasped. 'Malachy, you're a legend in Kilbeggin. I've heard great tales of you from the birds of the Swishtree Forest.'

'So you must be the man we saw at the cathedral in Kilbeggin,' said Kerry, slowly appearing from her hiding place. 'And we saw you again on the ship. But why did that eagle attack you and why are you here?'

Malachy smiled. 'My job is to protect the passengers on

board the Ark of Dun Ruah and to keep an eye on Red Beak and his horde. Red Beak doesn't live quietly here on Eyrie Island. He is laying plans to expand his kingdom. No place is safe from his evil eyes. I'm working with the Abbot. He's very concerned about what's going on out here. And you two have created quite a stir with your fireworks and laughing gas. Red Beak is quite annoyed.'

'I tried to stop her,' said Pod.

'I had to do something,' said Kerry. 'It was the only way we could get out of there.'

'It served its purpose,' said Malachy. 'But I've come to bring you news of your brother, Simon, and your friends, the swiftails. They are here in the Abbey searching for you.'

Kerry and Pod were delighted to hear that Simon was safe and the swiftails were on the island.

'Please take us to them,' they begged Malachy.

'The eagles are combing the Abbey for you right now,' he warned. 'You are in great danger. Red Beak is in very bad humour. I'm going to help you escape. But first I'm putting you under cover.'

'Under cover!' they exclaimed.

'I want you to hide under my cloak. This way the eagles won't see you.'

The Messenger pulled back the folds of his grey cloak to reveal a dazzling silver lining inside. He raised the cloak from his shoulders and tossed it over Kerry and Pod's heads. It billowed out and swirled down to cover them in a soft, sparkling sheath. Kerry felt a tingling sensation, shimmering over her skin.

'Just stay under my cloak and follow my footsteps. You won't be seen. We will be mere shadows to the eagles.'

Malachy led them through the library, back down the spiral staircase to the large circular room on the ground floor. They passed through a marble hallway and out through its front door. Here they encountered many flocks of eagle guards, patrolling the Abbey grounds. To Kerry's surprise, they passed by without being noticed. Wrapped in Malachy's cloak, she and Pod remained hidden from the eyes of their enemy. They followed him through the main courtyard, past the Great Hall and through the gardens to a little grove of oak trees. Malachy showed them to a hollow in the trunk of an old tree. They crept inside and sheltered.

'It's safe here,' said Malachy. 'Wait here for your friends.'

❂❂❂

Throughout the Abbey, the eagles were in turmoil. Red Beak arrived in the Great Hall with Queen Kiki at his tail. They were both in a rage after hearing of the disappearance of Kerry and Pod. Red Beak's anger deepened when he discovered the effects of the laughing gas on his henchmen. Roddick lined them up before him in the middle of the Great Hall. The six guards stood there, desperately trying not to laugh. Then one of them snorted and the others broke down into helpless hysteria. Turning to Roddick, the Eagle King demanded, 'Why are they behaving like this?'

'Something has gotten into them,' replied Roddick. 'I think

it's that recipe Queen Kiki ordered the prisoners to make. They must have drank it or inhaled it. It's had a strange effect on them. They appear to be drunk!'

At this the guards laughed even harder and one of them fell to the floor.

'Stop laughing, you idiots,' screeched Roddick. 'You can't even look after a girl and a decrepit old owl.'

'He isn't decrepit,' said Queen Kiki. 'He has a very good coat of feathers.'

'Exactly,' said Red Beak, 'and it's a very valuable coat of feathers. You lot will pay for this with your blood if they are not found straight away.'

Another outbreak of laughter emerged from the unfortunate guards, who then dissolved into lengthy fits of sneezing.

'You fools!' screamed Roddick, flying at the guards, his feathers standing on end. 'I'll strangle every one of you for this. And pluck every feather off your pathetic bodies. I can't believe that between all of you, you couldn't watch one girl and a neurotic owl.'

Roddick grabbed the nearest guard by the neck.

'Quiet, all of you,' ordered Red Beak. 'I must think. Let me concentrate.'

The King raised his right claw and stroked his crown feathers. His eyes turned deep crimson and gleamed like glowing embers. They sent beams of penetrating red light across the walls.

'I see two figures walking in darkness. They're in the cellars,' declared Red Beak. 'Search the cellars now.'

✪✪✪

When Niamh heard Queen Kiki ordering the guards to take Kerry and Pod to the tower, she decided to follow the secret passage from the fireplace in the Great Hall down to the kitchen cellars. Niamh knew that the prison tower was a new addition to the Abbey, built by Red Beak to torture his prisoners. There was no secret passage leading directly into the tower. But it was close to the library so she led Simon and the swiftails there. They made quick progress and were soon travelling along the main passage to the basement under the library when they heard the sound of eagles approaching.

'We've got to get out of this passage and into the library,' said Niamh. 'Hurry! We're not safe here.'

With the cries of the eagles echoing all around them, the little group tried to race faster but Red Beak's army was large and swift. They gained on them with every passing second.

Niamh ran ahead, with Simon and the swiftails following. Simon was on the lookout for something flammable that he could use to create a firework diversion and to frighten the eagles off. But the passages were damp, bare and empty and he found nothing useful.

The eagles were now right behind them. Simon hung back and threw a fistful of lit matches into the faces of the eagle guards. They fell back, screaming in pain as their feathers were scorched and charred. Simon shouted at Niamh and the swiftails to flee. He succeeded in holding the eagles off for several minutes while Niamh made it to the basement under the library and found what she was looking for. There was an opening into a narrow tunnel situated low down in the cave wall.

'Simon,' she screamed. 'Hurry Simon!' But all she heard was the flapping of eagles wings behind her. She slipped through the opening.

❁❁❁

While the strong eagle guards raided the underground passages the swiftails found a tiny crevice and hid there undetected. But Simon couldn't hide. He struggled against the strongest guards and flung lit matches at their eyes. But without any solid fuel to ignite he couldn't hold the eagles back for long. They swooped through the passage and captured him.

❁❁❁

Niamh was in an old tunnel that led from the basement up to the library. She scrambled over fallen rocks and stones, only to discover that the way was blocked before her. It was a dead end. The tunnel had either caved in or was blocked up by the eagles and she could go no further. The eagles tried to follow her into the tunnel but they couldn't stretch their wings in the cramped space. Afraid of being trapped, they gave up the pursuit. Niamh remained hidden behind some fallen rocks and the eagles finally retreated, thinking that she had escaped through the blocked tunnel.

After some anxious minutes waiting in silence Niamh figured it was safe to come out of the tunnel. She emerged from the opening to the tunnel whispering, 'Simon, Simon where are you?'

Suddenly, a dazzling light flooded her face. Her hands sprang up to protect her eyes. A large torch was flashed straight into her pupils, blinding her for a moment. A shadow lurked behind the torch. She saw the outline of an enormous eagle.

Taking to her heels, Niamh fled into the darkness. But the shadow followed. She raced blindly along the dark passages and caves.

'Where am I going?' she wondered, looking for landmarks along the way.

The eagle was about to overtake her. It flew over her head. By now she had lost her sense of direction. She turned into a narrow cavern and made for a low point where the roof almost touched the floor. Here she crouched. In this position the eagle couldn't swoop down on her from above. She grabbed a rusty candle stick that lay on the floor, and backed deeper into the crevice. The eagle darted towards her and she lashed out with the piece of metal, striking him on the wing. He screeched in pain and dropped the torch, swooping back out of her way.

Niamh picked up the torch and held it high. The eagle studied her.

'Who are you?' he demanded.

'Don't you dare come near me,' cried Niamh, 'or I'll kill you stone dead.'

'A nasty little piece of work, aren't you? Stay where you are then. You are trapped. And soon I'll be back with plenty of reinforcements.'

The eagle flew off and Niamh leaned back against the stone wall behind her to gather her strength. But, to her shock, the wall gave way and she fell down a steep shaft. She hit the ground with a crash. Bruised and dazed, she stood up and looked around her. She was still holding the torch.

Niamh saw that she was in a large tomb. Old stone slabs lined the walls and in the dim light she could see inscriptions on many of them. She shuddered. Through an archway she could see another tomb beyond.

'I must have stumbled into the catacombs under the cloisters,' she thought.

Niamh had never been in the catacombs. It was one place she had never dared to explore with Coleman. But she knew there was no point in trying to climb back up the shaft. It was far too steep. She also knew that the eagles wouldn't dare to follow her into the claustrophobic catacombs. So she tried to find a way through the labyrinth of tombs. A crunching sound under her feet caused her to freeze in her tracks. She shone the flashlight down and saw skulls and bones scattered beneath her.

'Human skeletons!' she screamed in terror.

The ground was littered with human bones. She kicked them aside and ran forward into the unknown. Speeding on blindly, she crashed straight into a wall, banged her head and fell to the ground. Her heart was racing and her head was spinning.

'I've got to calm down,' she thought, 'The only way that I'll get out of here is by keeping my wits about me.'

Composing herself with great effort, Niamh stood up and continued on until she came to a small crypt. She climbed a short flight of stairs and walked through a larger crypt which had a set of pews lined up the middle and a longer staircase at the other end. At the top of this stairs she arrived at a small wooden door.

Niamh tried the door but it was locked. When she examined it closely with the torch, she noticed that the lock had rusted. After a few hefty shoves it gave way and she stepped into a tiny chapel. She gasped in wonder as her torchlight hit the walls. They were decorated with magnificent frescoes.

Niamh was so relieved to be out of the tombs that she slumped down on the nearest pew and started to pray.

'Please, help me Lord,' she cried. 'Why did I get involved in this nightmare? It's such a terrible place. Oh please, please get me out of here; I don't want to see any more dead bodies.'

Then, she felt a hand on her shoulder.

CHAPTER 18

Eagles in Turmoil

Niamh stared at the hand on her shoulder. She spun around, ready to defend herself. A young monk in a brown habit stood before her.

'Niamh,' said the monk, his clear blue eyes shining. 'Niamh, thank God you're here.'

'Coleman!' gasped Niamh. 'Are you a ghost?'

'Of course I'm not a ghost,' he said, taking her hand in his.

Niamh felt the warmth flowing through her brother's hands. Tears welled up in her eyes.

'Coleman. You're alive! I can't believe it. Is it really you or am I losing my mind?'

'I'm as real as you are Niamh. Yes, I've been a prisoner here in the Abbey all this time.'

'I'm so glad that you're alive, Coleman. I've missed you every day since you disappeared. But the monks told us that you were dead. So did Red Beak.'

'When Red Beak discovered my manuscript work and realised how valuable it was he decided to keep me alive. He has kept me here working in solitude ever since. Only a small core of eagle guards know that I'm alive. They insist that I keep my face hidden under my hood at all times, especially when working in the library. My identity has been kept entirely secret. Usually there are eagles guarding me around the clock. But today they're preoccupied with other matters. So they've left me on my own. I work here from morning to night illuminating manuscripts. Red Beak sells them off for money and he's always demanding more. Sometimes he makes me work right through the night. But Niamh, tell me about you. What are you doing here in the Abbey?'

'I'm looking for a boy called Simon who came here searching for his sister and a Blue Owl who was kidnapped by Red Beak for his feathers. They were being held captive in the dungeons. But now they've been moved to the prison tower.'

'Yes, I saw eagle guards outside the tower earlier. And then I heard a lot of shouting and hysterical laughter. More guards arrived but now they're all gone. The prison tower is right beside us here. We can easily take a look.'

Coleman led Niamh through a narrow door at the side of the chapel. They emerged out into the monks' cloisters. They hurried through a series of archways skirting the enclosed cloister garden and made for the prison tower. Suddenly, Coleman stopped in his tracks and looked up towards the sky.

'Listen, I hear the sound of eagles flying,' said Coleman. 'Quick! We'd better go back to the chapel. It's safer there.'

As Niamh and Coleman ran back through the cloisters they saw it was too late. The eagles spotted them from the sky and quickly descended into the enclosed garden. Some of them landed at the chapel door, blocking their way. Another flock barred their way to the prison tower. The flocks started to close in on them from both sides.

'There's no way out!' said a voice beside them.

Niamh jumped. She turned to see a man in a grey cloak standing close to them.

'Just do as I say,' he commanded. 'Stand at my back, between those pillars.'

The man held his hands up high in the air. Niamh saw beams of white light radiating from his hands. A whirling wind rose and powerful gusts swept through the cloisters. Niamh was flung against one of the pillars. She wrapped her arms around it and clung on tightly. The eagle flock coming from the library side was swept up into the sky. The wind spun them around the Abbey walls in a powerful vortex, dashing them against the walls.

Then a mighty rumbling sound came from the chapel side. Niamh spun around to see eagles approaching and the roof of the cloisters collapsing over their heads.

The man in the grey cloak stood before her. His cloak swirled open and shielded her from the falling rafters. Blazing light emanated from the silver lining of his cloak, blinding her eyes and forcing her to cover her head. She fell to the ground and the floor beneath shook with the impact of the shattered roof. With cries of despair the eagle flock fell and lay buried beneath it.

Silence returned and the man in the grey cloak came forward and helped Niamh to her feet. Coleman was already standing beside him.

'Follow me,' ordered the man. Without knowing who this man was, Niamh was ready to trust him. He led them through the library door, past the great library halls and into a tiny room lined with ancient books. He reached out his hands to touch one of the bookcases and probed it with his fingers. Suddenly, his expression lightened. A smile lit up his lined face and brightened up the whole room.

'This is what I'm looking for,' he said.

Niamh could see that an almost invisible half-sized door was cleverly cut into the bookcase. The door swung open, revealing a flight of descending steps.

'Follow this pathway and it will lead you to safety,' he gestured.

'You must be the Messenger,' said Coleman. 'I'm so honoured to meet you. I've heard all about you. The monks hold you in the highest esteem.'

'Call me Malachy. And I am honoured to meet you both. But now you are in great danger and you must hurry. We will meet again soon and we will talk then. This passage is called Pilgrim's Way. It should be a safe escape route for you. It leads to the village of Coracle and when you get there you will find me waiting for you.'

'Yes, I know, it comes out at the old chapel on the cliff,' said Coleman. 'Is it still standing? I thought it might have fallen into the sea by now.'

'It's still standing,' said Malachy, 'but if another bad storm hits this island it may collapse. Now make haste. It's possible that Red Beak will find this passage and follow you. So go with haste.'

❂❂❂

Red Beak rose from his throne in the Great Hall and hovered over Simon. 'So you thought you could hide from me in my own home! You will never escape me. My eyes are all-seeing. My power is unbreakable. But now I command you to tell me where the rest of your friends are.'

'You claim to have all-seeing eyes,' challenged Simon, 'so you don't need me to tell you where they are, do you?'

'You try to be clever, boy. But you are playing with fire. My flocks will soon catch your friends. It's time to teach you a lesson you will never forget! Indeed, this will be your final lesson. Roddick, throw this prisoner into the tombs under the Abbey and bury him alive. Let him rot there with the corpses and skeletons in the Vaults of the Dead.'

Red Beak's blood-red eyes were liquid. Leaning forward, he hissed at Simon. 'You will die a slow and horrible death with only the rats to keep you company.'

Then he turned to Roddick. 'When you've locked him in the tombs, seal up the passages and make sure he doesn't get out. Now get him out of my sight.'

'Wait!' shrieked Kiki. 'What about the Blue Owl? Tell me where my owl is. I must have his feathers for my royal cloak.

And the girl with the fireworks, where is she? I'm still waiting for my firework display.'

'Oh, you mean Pod and my sister, Kerry,' shouted Simon.

'Yes,' cried Kiki, hopping up from her perch. 'Are you the brother who invented the matches?'

'Yes I am Simon, the inventor of Handy Matches, and I can create dazzling firework displays that will blow your mind. Let me entertain you.' He pulled a large orange match from his pocket and before anyone could stop him he struck it against the foot of Kiki's throne.

The throne burst into flames and Kiki shot up into the air screaming in fright. A flock of hens followed her. Smouldering black smoke swept high into the air. It swirled into a great thick cloud, forming a canopy over the Great Hall. The cloud burst. Deafening cracks of thunder erupted. Showers of scorching red sparks rained down on the room, flooding it with thick black smoke.

Stunned by the noise, the eagles froze. The burning red hail scorched their feathers causing them to scream in pain. Terrified eagles fled from the Great Hall. Red Beak rose screeching from his throne. Turmoil raged through the ranks of eagle guards as they tried to protect their master. A deep black smoke engulfed the room. It filled the atmosphere so thickly that everything turned black.

It was then that Simon heard a deep voice whisper in his ear. 'Your friends are waiting for you in the grove at the eastern side of the Abbey gardens. Look for the green gate. And hurry.'

Simon lit a blue match and used it to clear the thick fog

around his head. As the black fog parted, a clear path appeared before him leading straight to the door of the Great Hall. He hurried forward and pulled the door open, pausing for a moment to look back into the hall. Smoke had blackened the room completely. He hurried out into the courtyard and ran from the Abbey, across the gardens towards the grove at its eastern end.

To his great joy, Kerry, Pod and the swiftails were waiting for him under the cover of the trees.

Simon ran to embrace his friends. Pod flew straight onto Simon's shoulder and perched there chafing his neck in delight.

'Get off, you heavy creature,' said Simon, ruffling Pods big crop of blue feathers.

The swiftails flew in delighted circles around Simon's head.

'How did you two get here?' he asked.

'We heard a voice in the dungeons telling us that Kerry and Pod were out here waiting for us,' said Timmy.

'I heard a voice too. It must have been one of the good eagles that Browdan asked to help us ...'

'Look out – here come the eagles,' yelled Timmy.

Simon saw flocks of eagles rising from the Abbey. He scanned the grove for a way to escape. Then he remembered the words he heard in the Great Hall: *Look for the green gate.*

Straight away he spotted the green gate in the Abbey wall. 'Follow me through the gate,' he yelled at the others.

Kerry could see Pod struggling to fly as she followed Simon through the gate in the Abbey wall. The owl gasped for breath as the weight of his feathers strained his little body. With tremendous effort he tried to flap his heavy wings. But the effort was too much and he plummeted to the ground. Kerry reached out to catch him. She held him closely in her arms and ran. Simon and the swiftails ran ahead into the woodlands. Scores of eagles burst forth from the doors of the Abbey. Their angry screams tore across the sky as they searched for their prey.

Suddenly, two other eagles appeared ahead of them coming out of the woodlands. They swooped and before Kerry could jump out of his way, one of them seized her by the shoulders. He lifted her high up into the air and soared straight over the trees.

CHAPTER 19

Escape to Coracle

Kerry struggled to free herself from her eagle captor with Pod gasping in her arms. But he held her upper arms and shoulders firmly in his claws and carried her high over the woodlands. Soaring heavenward above the forests, they crossed the foothills that stretched westwards from where the Abbey stood between the two peaks. The eagle flew south following the course of a deep-flowing river. Kerry felt the cold evening breeze cutting through her limbs. She was still clutching Pod, who was panting heavily in her arms.

'Don't be afraid, Kerry!' said a familiar voice above her. To her great relief, she realised it was the voice of Grinwick, the security guard from the Ark of Dun Ruah. 'I've brought my brother, Farradore, with me to help you,' he said.

Kerry looked over her shoulder and saw another eagle carrying Simon. The swifttails were perched on his arm. Behind them a swarm of eagles blackened the sky. Red Beak's guards were in pursuit.

Grinwick followed the course of the river towards a valley. In the distance the Lone Peak Mountains rose high above its foothills. Kerry saw that a thick carpet of forest lay on either side of the river. But the pursuing eagles gained on them every second. Progress for Grinwick and his brother, Farradore, was slowed by the weight of their passengers. Red Beak's army was close behind them.

Kerry and Grinwick reached a bend in the river when a small flock of Red Beak's eagles caught up with them.

'We're not going to make it,' said Pod, who was fidgeting restlessly in Kerry's arms.

'We need to create a diversion. I'll lead them off in another direction.'

'No, Pod,' said Kerry. 'You're too weak. The weight of those extra feathers will pull you down.'

'I'll make for the forest,' said Pod. 'The trees will hide me.'

'I'm not letting you go.'

'But it's our only hope. It's me they're after, Kerry. I'm putting you in danger. With any luck the flock will follow me and you can get to safety.'

Before Kerry could stop him Pod burst from her arms.

'Whoot, whoot, whoot,' he called as he plummeted through the air.

The flock of pursuing eagles split in two. The larger flock went after Pod.

Grinwick made some ground after Pod broke from the group and quickly descended to the bank of a river. Farradore followed and they dropped their passengers at the edge of the treeline close to the river bank.

'We're going back to look for Pod,' said Grinwick. 'You must get under the shelter of the trees right now. The forest is thick here and the eagles won't be able to fly into it without catching their wings in the undergrowth. You will be safe if you stay close to the trees. If you continue on following the course of the river towards the Lone Peak Range you will see the deserted town of Coracle on the coast. Make for there and be sure to stay under cover. We will meet you on the outskirts of Coracle. Watch out for us. Quick! Red Beak's army is almost upon us again.'

As Grinwick and Farradore flew off a large group of eagles followed them into the distance.

The remaining flock swooped. Simon, Kerry and the swiftails rushed towards the forest. But the flock had already landed between them and the treeline. The eagles closed in on them, forcing them to retreat towards the river.

'Kerry! Swiftails! Help me gather firewood,' called Simon, gathering up clumps of twigs from the ground around him. They all joined in and quickly collected a large bundle. Simon used it to light a crackling fire. Eagle reinforcements arrived and swarmed over their heads. Then they started to circle around them and descend.

Simon dug a fistful of dirt out of the gravely riverbank behind him. He flung it into the fire. It spluttered and crackled, sending showers of hot sparks and embers spraying into the eyes of the birds that descended upon them. Screeching in pain, the eagles flew up into the air. Simon stirred the fire again and fanned it up to heighten the flames. Fiery darts shot high into the sky, striking scores of birds and scorching their wings. With terrified shrieks the entire flock rose in alarm and fled towards the Abbey.

'They'll be back', said Kerry, 'now that they know where we are.'

Running deep into the cover of the forest, they kept as close to the river as they could, following its course. They travelled through the afternoon until the light started to fade. Occasionally they stopped to drink from streams and to rest their tired feet. At last the trees started to thin out and they reached the foothills of the Lone Peak range on the southern tip of the island. As they crossed a small ridge they spotted a flock of eagles shadowing the sky. It was a larger flock than the first. Simon spotted a large rock that jutted out over the path. The little group of travellers hurried towards it and sheltered underneath.

'Don't make a sound,' whispered Simon as the flock passed overhead scanning the terrain below.

Simon, Kerry and the two swiftails lay under the large rock, holding their breaths in anticipation. The eagles flew on, scanning the forest with their laser-sharp eyes. As the danger passed by, the fugitives relaxed. They had escaped the evil eye of the enemy once again.

It was almost dark when the little group of travellers saw the dark blue sea glittering before them on the far horizon. On the coast lay the ruins of the deserted town of Coracle. The landscape in between was bare with a few rocky outcrops and parched bushes dotting the path that stretched before them to the town. They left the foothills, keeping a close watch out for eagles. As dusk deepened, the distant howling of jackals rose up around them. Staying under the cover of the few rocks and boulders they could find, they made for the deserted village of Coracle. But the cries of the jackals became louder and closer and they realised they were being followed by packs of wild dogs. The distance seemed vast and unending as they wearily trudged on.

Tired and thirsty, the bedraggled friends finally made it to the outskirts of Coracle with the jackals closing in behind them.

'Look over there,' said Timmy, pointing towards the sea. 'There are more eagles on the horizon and they seem to be patrolling the coastline and the cliffs.

'They're looking for us,' said Simon. 'We've got to find cover fast. Let's make for that old barn ahead.'

The howls of the jackals rose in a chorus as they reached the shelter of the old barn. They found the rickety wooden door unlocked and they gathered inside. Simon closed the door firmly behind them and set about finding beams and old barrels. He used them to bar the door. Then he kept watch from a gap under the roof of the barn while Kerry and the swiftails guarded the door.

'We're surrounded by jackals,' said Simon. 'I can see their eyes glittering through the darkness.'

Savage cries echoed around them as the wild dogs came

closer and closer. The leader of the pack lunged at the barn door trying to force his way through. Another jackal came forward to join him. Simon and Kerry threw their body weight against the door desperately trying to keep the dogs back. More jackals arrived and leaped, wildly clawing and scraping the splintering beams of the door.

'They're almost through,' cried Kerry.

'Hold on,' called Timmy. 'I can see two eagles coming. They look like Grinwick and Farradore. They're nearly here.'

The eagle brothers flew up to the barn and dived on the pack leaders. They sank their talons into their necks and pecked their ears. The leaders howled and the other dogs drew back in fright.

Inside the barn Simon found a wooden beam and set it on fire. He burst from the barn door brandishing it at the cowering animals. To his relief they scattered.

The eagle brothers hovered over the barn. They carried thick clumps of seaweed in their claws.

'Quench the torch with this,' cried Grinwick, throwing the seaweed to Simon, 'and get into the barn before Red Beak's scouts see you!'

The boy wrapped damp fronds of seaweed around the flaming torch and smothered the flames. He retreated into the barn followed by the eagle brothers and barred the door.

'We've brought you some bread and cheese,' said Farradore. 'Sit down and eat what you can. You must be starving.'

As they sat on the barn floor and ate the welcome food, Kerry asked the brothers about Pod.

'We found no trace of him,' said Grinwick. 'After we dropped you four off at the edge of the forest, we were followed by a large flock of eagles. We flew into the forest undergrowth and eventually managed to shake them off. Then when the coast was clear we returned to the river to look for Pod. We searched that whole area where he fell into the trees. But there was no sign of him anywhere.'

'I hope Red Beak's guards haven't found him!' said Kerry.

'We will continue to search for him,' said Farradore, 'but first we must carry out the Messenger's orders.'

'What orders?' Simon asked.

'He wants us to escort you to the cave village near Coracle where you can spend the night in safety with Browdan and his people.'

'Have you seen the Messenger yourselves?' asked Kerry.

'No. We met some of the free eagles in the forest a short while ago. They met the Messenger today and they gave us his message.'

'Thanks for coming back to the island, Grinwick,' Kerry said.

'Well, I felt pretty guilty after I left the two of you in the cellars of the Abbey. And when I returned to the ship I went straight to the Abbot and told him the whole story. Needless to say he wasn't too happy with me either. I felt responsible for leaving you here on your own at Red Beak's mercy. So I asked Farradore to come back with me. The Abbot gave us permission to help you. He asked us to search for the Blue Owl and help the Messenger to get you all to safety.'

'When we arrived on the island this morning', said Far-radore, 'the Messenger sent word to us that Kerry and Pod were hiding in the grove outside the Abbey. So we knew exactly where to find you. There are some good eagles in the Abbey being forced to work for Red Beak against their will. They are helping the Messenger and relaying messages back and forth. And they also sent you this bread and cheese.'

'Please thank them for us,' said Kerry. 'And we are so grateful to you both for helping us.'

'It's about time somebody stood up to Red Beak,' said Grinwick. 'But now you'd better finish up so we can take you to the sea caves. Then we can get back to our search for Pod.'

'But, what happened to Niamh?' Simon asked. 'Did she escape?'

'We don't have any news about Niamh,' said Farradore. 'No one has seen her so we think she escaped. When you reach the caves I'm sure you'll find her with Browdan, her brother. And he will have all the latest information. The Tawny Owl and many of the freebirds of the island are with him. They have their scouts out looking for Pod too.'

'But first we must get you to the cave village,' said Grinwick. 'And we must hurry. There's no time to lose. It's almost dark but eagles can see quite well in this light. Carry the clumps of seaweed we brought with us. You can use it as camouflage on your heads and shoulders. And watch out for eagle guards patrolling the skies.'

The little group made their way through the ruined village streets, covered in clumps of seaweed. They made it safely to a sandy beach and followed the coastline to a tall cliff face. All along the rugged shore dozens of shipwrecks lay dashed against the rocks. Their ghostly silhouettes cast long shadows under the bright silver moon.

'Why are there so many wrecks here?' Simon asked.

'This is the Sea of Sorrows,' said Farradore. 'It is treacherous. Many a ship has been blown off course and wrecked in the evil mists that fall along this coast.'

They reached some roughly hewn steps rising steeply into the cliff. Grinwick and Farradore directed the travellers to a narrow cave opening, almost hidden in the dark shadows of the rock face.

'This leads to Browdan's cave village,' said Grinwick. 'Hurry before more of Red Beak's patrols arrive.'

CHAPTER 20

The Troglodyte Village

Simon, Kerry and the swiftails slipped through the cave entrance that was hidden high in the cliff face. They found themselves walking through a narrow tunnel that descended into the rock and opened into a long succession of caves and passages. After the last trace of moonlight faded, Simon lit a match. He stopped to examine the walls. They gazed at the banded white and orange rock embedded in the high walls and ceiling of the vast cavern in which they stood.

'What beautiful colours,' Kerry exclaimed. 'It looks like this whole place is on fire.'

'Salt and iron oxide,' replied Simon. He was scraping the walls with his pocket knife and putting fistfuls of dust into his pockets.

'What are you doing?' Dot asked.

'This is perfect material for making explosives. It's an absolute goldmine for a pyrotechnic.'

'Is that all you can think about?' snapped Kerry. 'We're miles from home on this terrible island where Pod has been abducted and you're at it again … gathering salt and iron oxide for your crazy experiments!'

'Hey, there's no need to snap at me,' replied Simon. 'This stuff could come in very useful against those very same eagles who abducted Pod and—'

'Calm down you two,' soothed Dot. 'We're all tired and hungry from our long day of travelling.'

'But we need some kind of weapon to use against Red Beak and his hordes,' said Simon.

'Look!' interrupted Timmy. 'There's light ahead.'

A tiny sliver of light shimmered at the end of the next passage. The swiftails flew towards the light followed by Kerry and Simon. They found themselves at the entrance of an enormous cavern which was almost the size of a football pitch. Moonlight poured down from a huge opening in the roof. In the centre of the cavern a small lake reflected the light of bright, silver moonbeams throughout the giant cave.

A wide, grass verge swept around the edge of the lake. Cave dwellings were carved into the white marble walls of the cavern. Women stood outside brightly-painted doors that opened into their cave homes, chatting among themselves. Twinkling lights flickered through rounded windows that were cut out of the rock. The children were playing and laughing at the lake side in a little playground filled with wooden swings and slides.

Browdan emerged from one of the cave homes with a flock of birds at his shoulders and feet. He spotted the travellers and came with outstretched arms to welcome the visitors to his underground village.

'We have been waiting for you,' said Browdan as he wrapped his arms around them all. 'We're so sorry to hear that your friend Pod didn't make it here. He is a very brave owl to risk being captured by the eagle army to save his friends. We have sent word to all the freebirds on the island to search for him. If he is still hiding out in the forest they will track him down.'

'And what about Niamh?' said Simon.

'We think Niamh escaped but we have no details about where she is at the moment. She knows the Abbey like the back of her hand. I'm sure she'll be back here before long. But enough talk. Now it's time for you to eat and rest. The villagers have prepared a great meal for you. Come and make yourselves at home.'

Kerry, Simon and the birds were treated to a troglodyte's feast. They sat at a long table by the lakeside, eating and talking late into the evening.

'This is a magnificent cave,' Kerry told Browdan. 'It is so beautiful and yet it's all hidden underground.'

'The opening up in the roof of the cavern isn't entirely natural,' said Browdan. 'We have doubled its original size by hacking away at it. But it does let in lots of light, by day, which is healthy for the children.'

'But why haven't the eagles spotted this large hole from above?'

'They have. But there's a very strong air current coming down here. It's like a chimney with a downdraught. Some of the eagles have got caught in it and dashed into the lake where they were drowned. So they call it 'the black hole' and keep well clear of it. We also have some tricks of our own to scare them off. When the children see a nosey eagle looking down they start hissing like snakes. That scares most of them away. Red Beak knows there are some people living in the caves but he doesn't see us as a threat. He probably thinks that most of us have died of hunger over the past few years. We keep ourselves very well hidden.'

❂❂❂

Late into the night Kerry, Simon and the swiftails sat by the lakeside. They shared their stories with the children and their parents and listened to the fascinating folklore and history of the ancient island of Dun Ruah. With all the islanders had been through, Kerry was amazed at how contented they were. Their lives were simple and they survived on the support of close friends and family bonds.

That night some of the families invited them inside to stay in the cave houses. The people had chiselled out beautiful rooms in the white rock and moulded themselves very cosy homes, all brightly-decorated and reflecting the light from the glittering lake. Grateful for the luxury of comfortable beds, the travellers slept soundly through the night.

❂❂❂

The next morning Browdan and the people of the cave village gathered together to offer their little group of visitors one of their boats to escape on.

'We can't leave here until we find Pod and Niamh,' said Simon.

'Malachy will find them,' said Browdan. 'We should have news from him shortly.'

'I'm not sure that I trust that man,' said Simon. 'I know you all speak of him with great respect and I haven't met him myself, but why is he being so secretive? Kerry says that he looks like the man who was creeping around the cathedral at Kilbeggin the night the eagle attacked him. Then he appeared on the Ark of Dun Ruah and every time I tried to talk to him he got away! It was very annoying! I think his behaviour is very suspicious. He could be one of Red Beak's spies. Did you ever think of that?'

'But look how he helped us escape from the Abbey,' said Kerry.

'Pod didn't escape, did he?' Simon remarked.

'Did someone mention my name?' said a voice behind them. It was the Messenger. And nobody had noticed his arrival.

'Malachy,' cried Kerry. 'You're here. And we were just talking about you.'

'Good things I hope,' he said, fixing a smile on Simon. 'I'm sorry this is not a social visit. I've come to bring you disappointing news. Red Beak has captured your friend Pod. His guards found him in the trees near the river. He was unable to fly with the weight of his feathers. There's bedlam up in the Abbey since you all escaped. Red Beak wants to murder all around him. You must all stay here for the moment until I discover more of what his plans are. I've also come to tell you some good news. Two of your friends are arriving at the old chapel in the village of Coracle. Perhaps you would go to meet them, Browdan?'

'It must be Niamh,' cried Dot and Timmy together, swooping up into the air in delight. Everyone laughed to see them rejoicing.

'But who is the other friend?' said Browdan. 'Malachy where are you?'

But there was no answer. The Messenger had already vanished into the shadows.

CHAPTER 21

Preparing for Battle

Niamh and Coleman reached the chapel at the ruined village of Coracle early in the morning. They had been walking through the Pilgrim's Way all night. True to his word, Malachy the Messenger was waiting for them in the chapel. He had already opened a secret trapdoor on the flagstone floor, hidden under the altar. Here they emerged tired and hungry. Malachy offered them some water and fruit as refreshment. Then the prophet was on his way again. He left them with a warning.

'Stay here until the cave people arrive to fetch you. And whatever happens, do not leave this chapel before they arrive.'

As Niamh and Coleman waited for the cave people, streams of morning light beamed down in shafts onto the walls of the chapel. The beautiful stained-glass windows of the church gave it a warm glow. They heard a tapping on the chapel door. Niamh looked through a small window to see who was outside.

'Take a look, Coleman,' she said.

Niamh watched him strain to look through the glass. A big smile spread over his thin face.

A voice came from outside, 'Niamh, if you are in there please open the door. Malachy has sent us to look for you. Hurry or we'll be seen.'

Niamh opened the door and Browdan stepped in.

Browdan gasped when he saw his brother Coleman.

'Oh thank God you're alive,' he cried. They both laughed and embraced and then searched one another's faces.

'I can't believe you are alive and looking so well,' said Browdan. 'Red Beak told us you were dead.'

'Red Beak is the master of lies,' said Coleman. 'His entire regime is based on fabrication.'

'Well, his regime is beginning to crumble,' said Browdan. 'But I have so much to tell you. Let's talk on our way to the cave village. We have five years of catching up to do, brother. It's time to get you home.'

✿✿✿

The next morning Browdan called the villagers together in the large cavern. He had received news from the freebirds.

'The eagles have attacked the people of the lake and some of the sea cliff settlements. They are trying to break down their defences. At present the cave people are holding them back. But it's only a matter of time before they come here and try to attack us. There are no reports of casualties yet but Cian, chief of the Lake People, says that his community are very vulnerable, living so close to the Abbey. They can only hold out for a short time.'

'It's time to stop that eagle,' interrupted Simon. 'How can such a crazy psychopath have everyone here under his control?'

'But he's a very clever psychopath,' said Browdan. 'Yes, it is time we faced Red Beak. And in the near future we will. The Messenger has sent word to me that Red Beak's camp is divided. Many of the eagles are tired of his tyranny. They might take the opportunity to join us if they see our show of strength.'

'What are you planning to do?' asked Coleman.

'I want to put an army together and march on the Abbey.'

'Have you told the Messenger about this?' Coleman asked.

'I'm not sure that I trust that Messenger,' said Simon. 'He keeps disappearing and never tells us what he's up to. He could be leading us into a trap.'

'So you don't trust me,' said a voice beside Simon.

Simon jumped when he saw Malachy looking at him with an impenetrable expression on his face.

'How do you keep appearing like that?' Simon asked.

The Messenger looked thoughtful.

'A wise man watches and listens,' said Malachy. 'When he opens his mouth he speaks words of wisdom and truth. If you paid more attention to what was going on around you, you'd know a lot more about me.'

'Yes, but then you go and disappear again out of the blue. How on earth do you do it?'

'Watch and listen, Simon, and find out for yourself. A good

apprentice always observes his master.'

Simon looked puzzled.

'Are you saying that I should be your apprentice?'

'If your courage and dedication to your scientific experiments are anything to go by, I think you have the potential to be anything you want to be. And by the way, some of those shipwrecks you were looking at yesterday are full of explosives. Browdan has salvaged some from them already and hidden it in the caves. Fortunately, the munitions are dry and mostly intact. You will need to go onto the wrecks again to salvage whatever's left. There are plenty of old swords and daggers in there too.'

'Explosives on the shipwrecks … so you were watching us yesterday. I can't believe it. What kind of power do you have? Are you really a prophet?'

'You don't know me yet, Simon. And unfortunately you're still a boy with a lot of growing up to do. You have much to learn. It's time to lose your pride. Open your eyes, my boy. Stop hiding from the truth.'

Simon felt the green eyes of the prophet questioning him deep inside. It made him feel uneasy.

'But I came here about another matter,' said Malachy turning to Browdan. 'You plan to form an army and then march on the Abbey?'

'Yes,' said Browdan.

'You must wait until Grinwick and the birds of the forest have had time to influence more of Red Beak's eagles. Many of them are on the verge of fleeing from him. Red Beak has been punishing his guards with great cruelty. They are terrified. We need a little more time to persuade them to leave him. I'm asking you to trust me. But maybe that is too difficult for some of you.'

'I trust you, Malachy,' said Br Coleman. 'And I know who you are. You've always protected the monks of the Ark of Dun Ruah and the inhabitants of this island. You are a prophet of the highest order. We are blessed to have you with us.'

The villagers nodded their heads to show their support.

'I must warn you that you may not be safe here for long,' said Malachy. 'This is what I suggest you do to keep yourselves safe. The strongest among you should go back to the village of Coracle, set up camp there and take your old homes back. Try to build up some form of protection for the village. Make it your stronghold. It will be the fortress from which you can defeat Red Beak. It will also divert the eagles away from here. The children and the older folk can stay here under the protection of the caves.'

'It's not going to be easy,' said Browdan. 'We need everyone to support this.'

'Yes you will need the support of all the islanders. Cian and the lake people are with you. The good eagles and the freebirds of the forests are also willing to help in any way they can. Get them to spread the news of what you are doing to the other villages on the island.'

'And the monks on the Ark of Dun Ruah, will they support us?'

'The Abbot is with you. I believe he'll be here when you

need him. Now I must make a request. I need you to provide me with your best boat for a voyage I have to make.'

'What voyage?' Browdan asked.

'I'm leaving the island,' said Malachy.

'What?' cried Simon. 'How could you leave us now? You can't go off like this just when Red Beak is about to attack. Are you mad?'

The Messenger turned once more to Simon.

'Red Beak is preparing to attack,' he said, 'but he is clever enough to wait for the right moment. It will take some time for him to rally his troops and make an effective impact. I can be more useful by leaving the island. You must trust my judgement.'

'But what's all the secrecy about?' probed Simon. 'At least tell us where you're going.'

Malachy took a deep breath. 'I'm going to speak to the Abbot on board the Ark of Dun Ruah. He is very keen to be kept up to date on the events that are occurring on the island. And he is very upset about the fact that Pod was kidnapped on his own ship. He wants to do everything in his power to help him.'

'But it's not the Abbot's fault that Pod was kidnapped,' said Kerry.

'I know,' said Malachy. 'But he feels responsible for the passengers on his ship. Also many of the monks would like to come back to live on the island. They've had enough of floating around the ocean. They want to be monks not sailors, cleaners and cooks. Some of them are trying to put pressure on the

Abbot to lend his support to the battle against Red Beak. I hear he's on the point of giving in to the wishes of the younger monks. They have asked me to lend my influence.'

'You have my blessing, Malachy,' said Browdan. 'Come with me and I'll find a good boat for you.'

'Can I come with you, Malachy?' Br Coleman asked. 'I might be able to help you persuade the Abbot.'

'But why do you need a boat?' Simon asked. 'You are a prophet of the highest order. Surely you don't need a boat to get there. Why don't you use your magical powers?'

Malachy laughed. 'Don't you know that strong magic is like strong alcohol, Simon? An overdose can leave you with a hangover that lasts for days, sometimes months. I don't use magic.'

'But what about all the times you escaped me?'

'Maybe you're not as observant as you should be,' said Malachy. 'A master of discretion can fade into the background when he wants to. I use the elements of nature like the wind to help me travel faster, or shadows to hide in. But I have been blessed with gifts from one much greater than me. And these gifts I only use in times of great need. Red Beak is quite a formidable opponent. I need to keep my strength to deal with him.'

❂❂❂

Kerry sat on the sea wall watching the islanders prepare the boat for Malachy and Coleman. Malachy was already on board. He waved at Kerry and she waved back. He studied her for a moment. Then before she knew it, he was out of the boat and at her side.

'Something is troubling you Kerry. What is it?'

'Oh, I'm sorry for looking so sad, Malachy. But I feel that I have put everyone in danger by taking them on this trip. If I had taken Pod's advice we would still be back in Kilbeggin. And Pod would be safe. But I do need to make a living. How am I going to save our home and take care of Simon without a decent income?'

'You are carrying a heavy burden right now, my child. But in time this will grow lighter and turn to great good. Your experiences here will strengthen both you and Simon and draw you closer together. I can offer you and Simon a passage on this boat with me right now back to the Ark of Dun Ruah and onwards to the Land of Fire. You can trust Browdan and the islanders to find your friend Pod. Do you want to come with me now?'

'And leave Pod on the island? I'd never do that. No, I want to stay here and help the islanders too. In the last few days I've really grown to love those people. But, you know, I miss my mother right now. I feel so alone at times like this. I wish I had someone like you to guide me.'

'I'm glad you have chosen to stay Kerry. Sometimes we have to face our enemy and fight. And it can be very lonely. But remember that this too will pass away. All struggles and sorrows pass eventually. They make us better people.'

'Do you have to leave us, Malachy?'

'I will never leave you, Kerry. I will always be your friend.

All you have to do is call my name and I will be with you. I promise you that.'

Malachy boarded the little sailing boat the islanders had prepared for himself and Br Coleman. Kerry looked out to sea and watched them sail away. She hoped that they would return safely with help.

❁❁❁

After Malachy and Coleman had left the island, Browdan sent his friend the Tawny Owl as a messenger to the birds of the forest. Soon the news of the rise against Red Beak spread to every corner of the island. The birds came and held a great conference with him on the cliff edge near the sea caves. Eagles, owls, hawks and all the smaller birds pledged to band together with the cave dwellers to overthrow Red Beak and his army. They left to spread the word to all the cave villages on the island.

All through the night a procession of young men and women left their caves on the coast and by the lake. They walked to Coracle carrying with them whatever weapons and tools they could find. Arriving in droves to the little town, they sang ancient battle songs.

We shall eat our bread to the full,
And dwell in our land in safety.
We will live in peace and lie down,
And none will make us afraid.
We will rid the land of evil beasts.
We will chase our enemies down.

They will fall before us in their thousands.
We will put ten thousand to flight.

Browdan set up his headquarters in the old town hall in the centre of the village. The people moved in to repossess the houses in the town. They restored the roofs and walls and strengthened the windows and doorways to make them into impregnable fortresses. That day the villagers worked openly for the first time since Red Beak's reign of terror began. They cut down wood from nearby forests and dragged it into the village for the making of furniture and tools. They carried great stones into the town from the barren lands and used them for building purposes. They laboured long hours, rebuilding their homes and their village. The ironmonger lit up his old furnace to forge weapons, helmets and shields. The baker cleaned up his ovens and baked fruit and potato bread for the workers.

❂❂❂

The following day, Red Beak's scouts started circling the town. They kept a distant watch on what the local people were doing but they didn't attack. Everyone had begun to relax and they were making great strides in restoring their village. They went about their work with new confidence, openly laughing and singing for the first time in five long years.

Suddenly, the bell on the town hall rang out. The people flocked to its doors. There stood Browdan with Cian, the chief of the Lake People, Niamh and Grinwick were at his side.

They all waited for Browdan to speak.

CHAPTER 22

Ring of Fire

The islanders and the freebirds had responded to the toll of the bell. They flocked to listen to what Browdan had to say. Simon, Kerry and the swiftails stood with them to offer their support.

'Red Beak has gathered together a great army of eagles,' said Browdan. 'Grinwick has just got word that they are about to attack our town and to crush us once and for all. Unfortunately, we are not ready to face them yet. We have no battle strategy and not enough weapons. So the only thing we can do is lock ourselves into our homes and defend the work we've done already as best we can. That's unless someone here has a plan.'

'I have,' shouted Simon. 'I've got a plan.'

'Speak up then if you do,' said Browdan.

'We can use fire to frighten the eagles off,' said Simon stepping forward. 'With the help of the people of this town I can make enough fire to terrify the wits out of those eagles.

Red Beak's flocks are afraid of fire. I've seen with my own eyes how they react to it. If they see that we are not afraid of them they will lose confidence. Let's show them that we won't be beaten.'

Some of the villagers shouted their approval.

'You haven't seen what those eagles are capable of, Simon,' said Browdan.

'Yes I have,' replied Simon. 'When I was captured and brought before Red Beak's throne in the Abbey, I confronted them with fire. They went crazy with fear. And when they chased us to the riverbank near the forest I threw fire at them again. It worked. They screamed with terror and the whole flock fled back to the Abbey. I know we can do this.'

'But you have only dealt with them in small numbers up to now, Simon,' said Cian. 'How can you possibly make the fire big enough to scare an entire army?'

'We can build a ring of fire around this entire town. Fire spreads rapidly so it won't take very long to get it going. First we'll send people out in every direction armed with my matches, and with fuel and explosives. We'll build a circle of fires dotted around the edges of the town. Then we'll link them together to form a huge unbroken ring.'

'But where are we going to get all the explosives?'

'I have worked with pyrotechnics for years. And since I've arrived on the island I've been collecting minerals from the underground rock. I've never seen such a wealth of raw material for making explosives. And I have gathered enough material by now to blow Red Beak off the planet. We'll make that ring of fire so hot and dangerous that Red Beak won't come back for a long time.'

'I think we should give Simon a chance,' interrupted Grinwick. 'What have we got to lose? We can always resort to Browdan's plan and run for cover if it doesn't work.'

'Let's put it to a vote,' said Browdan. 'All in favour of Simon's plan shout now.'

With a great roar the entire village shouted their support for Simon's plan.

'It looks like we're with you, Simon,' said Browdan. 'But the eagles could be on their way. How fast can you build this ring of fire?'

'Well, how much time have we got before they get here?'

'They were swarming over the Abbey preparing to leave when I left there,' said Grinwick. 'They could be here within the hour.'

'We can do it if everyone pitches in,' said Simon. 'Listen to the plan.'

Simon stood beside Browdan giving orders to the hundreds of men and women who came forward to volunteer for the various tasks involved.

Cian led a band of villagers to the edge of the town to gather firewood from the forest. Browdan built an enormous bonfire in the square in front of the town hall. The people brought torches to the bonfire and set them alight. They used the torches to light more bonfires in the streets and at the edge of the town. Within minutes a circle of small fires were dotted close together around the perimeter of the town.

During his few days in the underground cave village, Simon had dug out a substantial store of salt and iron oxide from the rock to use as ingredients for making explosives. He enlisted the help of a team of volunteers to make batches of simple firearms and fireworks. They swung into action and distributed the explosives among the villagers for use when the signal was given. Browdan sent another team to the shipwrecks to collect some of the remaining munitions on board.

Within the hour Red Beak's eagles were circling over the town. Company after company arrived, darkening the sky with their outstretched wings. Simon's action plan was ready to roll out. Browdan's volunteer army awaited the signal.

'Launch the flare,' Browdan ordered.

Simon launched a white flare from the old cannon at the town hall which rocketed straight into the eagles' midst. It exploded with a mighty crack, scattering the eagles from left to right. At this signal, the villagers detonated their missiles and quickly retreated under cover. Simon's first range of fireworks shot up into the heavens and burst into flaming showers followed by loud thunderclaps. Hundreds of eagles fled across the sky, fanning the flames with their wings. The flames grew higher, scorching their tails and burning their feathers.

Screaming with fright and pain, the eagle flocks fled from their position above the centre of the town. They flew to the outskirts where the ring of bonfires lay. Here Browdan's allies, the freebirds, lay waiting, hidden in the scrublands surrounding the town. They were armed with small grenades. At the signal they flew high up to the sky and dropped the grenades into the outlying fires. The explosions rocked the landscape and fires leaped high into the air. Spreading rapidly, the flames joined to form an unbroken circle of fire as a shield around the town. A fierce heat rose from the ring of fire high up into the air, scorching the great birds. Red Beak and his generals screeched orders to their forces to retreat. His entire army flew eastwards with shrill screams. Crestfallen, they returned to the Abbey. Red Beak had lost his first battle.

❂❂❂

That evening Browdan met with Simon, Kerry and Niamh, the leaders of the cave settlements and the freebirds of the island. 'It's time for us to lead an attack on the Abbey,' he said. 'Have I got your support?'

There was full agreement among all the parties.

'We're going to need more ammunition to attack the Abbey,' said Simon.

'I'll send a team of volunteers into the underground tunnels to dig out more minerals for you,' said Cian. 'Just tell us what you need.'

'And I'll send another team onto the shipwrecks to salvage the remaining explosives,' said Browdan.

❂❂❂

Later in the day Browdan called a public meeting at the town hall. Hundreds of islanders arrived to volunteer their support.

'We plan to march on the Abbey tomorrow,' Browdan announced to the new recruits. 'The time has come to show our strength against Red Beak's forces. We have decided to call ourselves the White Army.'

The crowds cheered.

'Go and find anything you can to use as armour and weapons to take with you on the march,' he ordered. 'Cover your heads and shoulders with helmets and shields. And may God go before us!'

'May God go before us,' roared the people.

By nightfall over a thousand people had already arrived in Coracle to join the uprising against Red Beak. The word spread and hundreds more arrived during the night from the sea caves and the hill caves. The White Army grew.

Simon and his assistants worked throughout the night creating a firearms factory inside the town hall. He had already trained up a team of competent technicians to construct and manufacture large batches of smoke bombs, exploding missiles, grenades and thunder rockets.

Kerry and the villagers made brightly-coloured banners, painted with giant orange flames, to frighten the eagle army. They painted their faces with warpaint made from coloured chalks from the sea cliffs. Every scrap of old metal was used to weld helmets, swords and shields together. The swiftails joined the freebirds as messengers. They sent word to the free eagles and other creatures on the island in an effort to persuade them to join the White Army.

Just after dawn flocks of Red Beak's eagles started to circle the town of Coracle once again. This was a setback for Browdan. He sent for the freebirds and the leaders. They met in the town hall to make fresh plans.

'What are those eagles doing back here already?' said Browdan. 'I thought they would stay away for longer than this after the scorching they got yesterday.'

As he spoke the Tawny Owl and the freebirds arrived to join them in the town hall. Their spies had just informed them of the latest news about Red Beak.

'Red Beak has left the Abbey,' said the Tawny Owl. 'It is completely deserted. My sources tell me that he has set up camp in Cooley House.'

'Oh no!' cried Niamh. 'How could he do this?'

'Where is Cooley House?' Simon asked.

'It was once our family home,' said Browdan. 'It was where we lived as children with our parents. The house lies about a mile outside the village. Niamh and I have always hoped that one day we would return there and restore our old home.'

'We've just been informed that the eagles are using it as a base from which they plan to attack the town,' said the Tawny Owl. 'Now their forces are arriving in convoys and surrounding the outskirts of the Coracle. My spies in Red Beak's camp have told me they plan to occupy the outlying fields and forests and lay siege to us.'

'That means we can't go ahead with our plan to march on the Abbey,' said Cian. 'Doing so would invite attack from both Cooley House and the Abbey. We will have to remain close to the confines of the town.'

'Then we will surprise them by marching on Red Beak's camp in Cooley House,' said Browdan. 'It is much closer than the Abbey and we know it well. But we must move quickly. There is nothing like a surprise attack.'

'Yes,' agreed Simon, 'and it won't be long before those eagle scouts have us completely surrounded. We've got to go now!'

'Go and gather the White Army together,' commanded Browdan.

CHAPTER 23

The White Army

Red Beak's guerrilla forces gathered in large flocks around the town of Coracle. They started another series of quick raids on the town. Flocks landed on the rooftops and perched there waiting to attack the townsfolk. Then they descended on people in the streets using their old tactics of pecking necks and shoulders from the air. They forced their victims back into their houses.

Browdan and the leaders reacted quickly. They sent out the freebirds to rally the White Army to assemble at the town hall. In full force they came armed with torches of fire to defend themselves against the marauding eagles. People were angry at the eagles' tactics and arrived wearing makeshift helmets and carrying swords, axes and spears. They sang battle songs and chanted war cries in anticipation of the battle.

'The White Army is ready,' declared their chief, Browdan. 'We will march on Red Beak's camp in Cooley House and we will drive them out before us.'

The army cheered and raised their weapons shouting, 'We will drive them out before us.'

'Arm yourselves with every weapon you can find and carry a lighted torch. Shield your heads because we'll face more eagle air raids on the way. Simon will distribute fresh missiles to all of you. We will launch another attack on Red Beak's sky patrols shortly. Wait for the signal. Prepare to march and do so with courage, confidence and strong hearts. We will prevail against our enemy.'

'We will prevail!' roared the White Army.

Browdan gave the signal to his army to detonate fresh batches of grenades and missiles at the eagle patrols from strategic points around the town. Searing hot flames shot across the sky followed by deafening claps of thunder. The terrified eagles scattered. Many of them were forced to retreat to Cooley House and regroup behind its gates and walls.

Browdan's White Army was now ready to march. The freebirds remained on the outskirts of the town armed with grenades and ready to defend the town in his absence. At his signal, the army set out from the village of Coracle to the great home of the old chief of the island. Waving Kerry's fiery banners and armed with explosives, grenades, swords and daggers, the islanders sang and cheered as they marched. They wore colourful helmets and shields to protect their heads and shoulders from the eagles. Before long they arrived at Cooley House. Red Beak's eagle sentries were perched high on the walls and stood ready to attack. The old wooden gates had been restored and were now barred shut before them.

'Set fire to the gates,' ordered Browdan.

Simon hurled a grenade at the gates and soon they were blazing high.

A shrill chorus of war cries could be heard rising from inside the grounds of the house. As the gates caved in they could see flocks of eagle warriors congregating on the rooftop of the old house. Then, with piercing battle cries, the eagles flew up into the air and formed a huge swarm, which, like a huge dark rain cloud, blackened the sky as it flew towards Browdan's army that stood waiting at the burning gates. Simon went into action feeding the fire and raising it higher. The swarm of eagles flew over the gate, ready to pounce on their prey. They were hit by a mass of fire missiles. The White Army's front line sprayed the skies with balls of fire as line after line of eagles approached.

With screams of anguish, scores of eagles were brought down. The rest scattered in shock, their feathers singed by the terrible heat. Most of them flew straight back to Cooley House. The others flew towards the forest.

'Force the gates!' cried Browdan.

The White Army ran at the gates and battered them with their weapons. Burning shards of wood fell to the ground and the gates quickly crumbled. They marched up the driveway to the door of the old chieftain's home and surrounded the house. Chanting and shouting fierce war cries, they brandished their torches at the eagle guards. Browdan's men stormed the front door and he entered the house with Simon and Cian at his side. There, at the end of the entrance hall, were Red Beak and Queen Kiki sitting on two makeshift thrones. Roddick and their cronies surrounded them.

'This is as far as I will allow you to go, Browdan!' cried Red Beak. 'Stop this foolishness and go back to your cave. You know you are not fit to rule this island. You wouldn't stand a chance without that trickster Simon and his fireworks. What do you know about armies and warfare? All you are is a filthy troglodyte. You are weak, like your father before you. And this island is mine!' His red eyes gleamed as he spat out the words.

'And you, Red Beak,' replied Browdan, 'what power do you have except the power you stole from my father when you murdered him? You tortured him and robbed him of his position as chief of the island. And now you have the nerve to sit in his house, on his chair, wearing his sapphire ring.'

'That's a lie!' hissed Red Beak. 'Your father ran away from the battle and caused his own downfall. He couldn't defend himself. He was always a coward. And you are nothing but a fool. Look at your military chief. He's only a little boy playing with fireworks.'

'My father was a great chieftain. And you are a murderer and a liar.'

'What?' interrupted Queen Kiki. She flew off her perch and stood before her husband glaring at him. 'Did you actually murder the chief of the island?'

'I told you he was a coward. He brought it upon himself.'

'You never told me anything about this,' said Kiki. 'I would never have married you if I thought you were a usurper. You always told me that you had rightfully ascended to the throne. You said you were a man of peace.'

'Shut up, you foolish hen,' Red Beak ordered. 'What do you know about my affairs? All you're interested in is feather parades and jewels. If it wasn't for your insatiable desire for cloaks made from royal-blue feathers we wouldn't have this uprising on our hands. Remember I brought the Blue Owl here for you.'

'How dare you speak to me like that! I've had nothing but trouble since I came to this island to marry you.'

'I give you everything you ask for,' said Red Beak, 'and still you're not happy. Nothing is good enough for you. Get yourself and your hens out of here and stop interfering in my business.'

'You've gone too far this time, Red Beak,' cried Kiki. She rose from the ground in a flurry of feathers and called for her hens to follow her. And before Red Beak could stop her, she had flown through a gap in the roof. Hundreds of her loyal servants and friends went with her. They flew through the roof of Cooley House and high up into the air, escaping the White Army that surrounded the house. Led by Queen Kiki, they fled to the mountains.

Red Beak looked crestfallen.

'You're finished, Red Beak,' said Browdan. 'Your army is divided so you might as well flee yourself. Why don't we end this peacefully? Go after your Queen.'

'But first tell us what you've done with the owl,' cried Simon.

'Never,' screamed Red Beak. 'Kiki will be back for the owl's feathers. She knows she can't survive without me. She always ck.'

counting your chickens,' said Browdan, 'because
e they will not hatch. Let's face it, Red Beak, your
power is broken. We don't believe your foolish lies and we don't
fear you. Soon the monks from the Abbey will return and
take possession of their rightful home. Your days here are num-
bered.'

'You're just like your father,' said Red Beak. 'You're full of
empty talk but underneath it all you're weak. No Cooley will
ever get the better of me.' Red Beak suddenly rose from his
throne.

'Roddick, Guards, block the door,' he screeched.

'This won't work,' said Browdan. 'We've got you surrounded.
A bonfire is blazing outside. If you don't let us go my army will
set fire to the house.'

'What? And kill us all inside, including you and your top
generals? Are your men really that stupid? Face the facts,
Browdan. You're trapped. Roddick! Seize these imbeciles
and tie them up. That army outside won't last long with the
ringleaders all locked up in here.'

Simon acted swiftly. Before the guards could seize him,
he flung a fire grenade high up into the air. It hit the ceiling,
exploded with a series of cracks and burst into a shower of
spluttering fireballs. The hissing fireworks zigzagged in bursts
across the room, scorching the eagles like red dragons of fire.
Red Beak's guards flew up in a swarming frenzy of blood-
curdling screams. The illusion looked so real that they believed
they were being attacked by real dragons. In a rush of

confusion they fled to the door of Cooley House and burst through to the outside. They flew to the east.

Red Beak and Roddick were left alone. Slumped over his perch, Red Beak glared at Browdan and his friends with his red eyes blazing.

'If you think your clever tricks can frighten me then you're making a very big mistake. You may think you've won this small battle but you'll never have a moment's peace while I still live on this island. I'll be back tomorrow with an even greater army. Don't forget I still have the owl, hidden far away from here. You'll never find him. Come on, Roddick.' He flew up into the rafters followed by his loyal servant.

'I'll have my day,' shouted Red Beak, disappearing through the roof.

CHAPTER 24

Queen Kiki's Crystal Chamber

The next day Red Beak's loyal eagles returned to scan the skies over the village of Coracle. The freebirds under the leadership of the Tawny Owl kept a keen watch on them throughout the morning. The White Army worked hard to repair the damage to the town and build up its defences. Simon was busy with his team of technicians creating fresh stores of explosives.

At noon Grinwick, Farradore and the swiftails arrived at the town hall. They met with Browdan, Cian, Kerry and Niamh.

'Red Beak is already planning a fresh attack,' Grinwick said. 'The Eagle King has moved back to the Abbey with flocks of loyal supporters. He has sent Roddick and his generals out to bully the scattered flocks. Most of them are still so afraid of him that they are now returning meekly to the fold.'

'And where did Queen Kiki go?' Kerry asked.

'Queen Kiki has set up a camp of her own. It's composed mainly of her servants and friends but she has quite a large following. They have made their base high up in the Lone Peak Mountains north of the village of Coracle. Other flocks have deserted both the King and Queen. They are hiding in the mountains and forests. Many of these are liaising with the freebirds of the island. Significant numbers of them are joining the side of the freebirds and the White Army. Our spies tell us that Red Beak is expecting that Queen Kiki will come back to him. Unfortunately, his power is not broken.'

'I don't think Queen Kiki is all bad,' said Kerry. 'Red Beak was right when he said she was spoilt and foolish but I don't think she's evil. Maybe somebody should try and talk to her. She might know where Pod is.'

'I was just about to get to that,' said Grinwick. 'My sources think that Queen Kiki has the Blue Owl with her in the Lone Peak Mountains.'

'Then I'll have to go to see her,' said Kerry. 'I feel so guilty about bringing Pod along on this trip when he never wanted to come in the first place. And I can't bear hanging around waiting for news. I want to do something to get him back.'

'It's dangerous, Kerry,' said Browdan. 'Those mountains are treacherous to climb.'

'I'll come with you,' said Niamh. 'I know the Lone Peak Mountains. There are many tunnels and caves in the mountain that might be useful if we need to get under cover. We could also bring some of the freebirds with us to scout before us.'

'Count me in,' said Grinwick. 'I know the Lone Peak well. And I know the swiftails won't let Kerry out of their sight so we'd better include them too.'

'Of course, we'll come with you,' agreed Timmy and Dot.

'I suppose it's worth a try,' said Browdan, 'but Simon may not be too happy when he hears about this.'

'We'll go before he tries to stop us,' said Kerry.

'Go ahead and make your preparations then,' said Browdan, 'and I'll try to keep Simon busy.' Then Browdan turned to Grinwick.

'Before you leave me, have you got any further news about Red Beak?' he asked. 'Do you have any idea what he is planning next?'

'We don't have any information on what plans Red Beak and his generals are hatching at the moment,' said Grinwick. 'This time Red Beak is keeping his cards very close to his chest. He is communicating exclusively with Roddick and his closest commanders. But we have many spies on our side now.'

'We expect to have some news soon,' added Farradore.

'What do your freebirds advise me to do now?' Browdan asked.

'Keep working on building your artillery and devise a better way of defending the town,' said Farradore. 'The weather is changing so Simon's skills in pyrotechnics may not be effective. You'll have to develop a contingency plan.'

'Why do you say the weather is changing?' Simon asked as he walked into the room. 'There's not a cloud in the sky.'

Farradore sighed.

'Simon, you have a lot to learn about the weather on this island,' said the eagle. 'Things can change in the blink of an eye. I hear that fireworks don't work too well in the rain. I was just saying that you will need to work on developing more heavy artillery.'

'Fireworks and explosives can work in any kind of weather', said Simon, 'but it's a bit more complicated. And it depends on what chemicals you put into them. I'll see what I can do.'

'That will keep you busy, Simon,' said Browdan. 'We need to make plans for defending the town but we must also get ready to attack. Farradore, when are you returning to the Abbey foothills?'

'I will go now.'

'Then send word to us as soon as you get any news about Red Beak's plans.'

❖❖❖

Kerry, Niamh, Grinwick and the swiftails set out for the Lone Peak Mountains early in the afternoon. Simon got wind of Kerry's journey and tried to dissuade her from undertaking it. But she stood her ground. She was determined to see Queen Kiki and to persuade her to release Pod. And she also wanted to invite the Queen to join the White Army and plead with her husband to return the island to its people.

They left the village of Coracle wearing camouflage and carrying enough food and provisions for the next day. Their first task was to cross the barren lands that lay between Coracle and the Lone Peak Mountains.

Through the afternoon Kerry heard the cries of the wild dogs and eagles in the distance. By evening they had reached the foothills of the Lone Peak Mountains. Niamh led the climb to the central Lone Peak, where Grinwick said the Eagle Queen had made her camp.

In the light of the fading sun Grinwick spotted a flock of eagles high on the Lone Peak. He took the swiftails with him to scout. Kerry and Niamh were left alone. The path had grown narrow and the climb was rocky and steep. The cries of the wild dogs were getting closer. A chill wind blew up around them. Kerry saw that they had reached what looked like a sheer cliff. It loomed high over their heads.

'We've got to scale this rock face, Kerry,' said Niamh. 'Stay close to me and do exactly what I say. Don't worry, I'll keep you safe. Oh, and try not to look down.'

Kerry looked up at what appeared to be a vertical overhang.

'There are footholds all the way up to the top,' said Niamh. 'I climbed this with Coleman when we were children. It is much easier than it looks. When we get to the top there is a tunnel that will take us higher. We will have shelter there and find warmth in the caves.'

Kerry followed Niamh closely and was glad that darkness had set in. She was grateful that she couldn't see how high they had climbed and how far the drop was below her. The howls of the wild dogs had faded away and she knew the clifftop was close.

'Here, take my hand,' said Niamh. 'We're almost there.'

Niamh and Kerry scrambled to the top and rested there looking out over the starlit sky with the glimmering sea in the distance.

'It's beautiful,' said Kerry. 'I love how the stars light up the sky and the ocean at night. But look, Niamh, what are those lights moving towards us?'

'The eyes of the jackals!' exclaimed Niamh. 'And they are close. Hurry Kerry! We must run for the tunnel.'

The jackals started howling again as they drew closer to the girls. Kerry heard them panting behind her. She turned to see a large pack of hungry-looking dogs close at her heels.

'Run, Niamh,' she cried.

The jackals chased the girls up the mountain path. Kerry felt a sharp pain in her ankle. It felt like it was going to give way under her weight and she was forced to limp. She saw that she was losing ground behind Niamh.

'I can't make it much further,' she called. 'I hurt my ankle back in the Abbey and it's started acting up again.'

To her relief, Grinwick and the swiftails appeared on the path before them. The eagle swooped at the wild dogs with a shrill, piercing cry and they retreated into the shadows. Then he returned to Kerry and Niamh.

'We've spoken with Queen Kiki's guards,' said Grinwick. 'She has agreed to talk to you. There is not much further to go to the eagles' base. I'll go ahead of you. Just keep moving.'

Grinwick flew off and Kerry tried to run on her ankle again. It had been weak ever since she fell against the tapestry wall in the Abbey, the day she arrived on the island.

To her horror the ankle gave way again on the difficult mountain terrain. She lost her footing and tumbled down the rough incline, straight into the path of the jackals. Scrambling back up the path, she came face to face with a hungry wild dog.

The dog bared his long fangs and growled.

'Get away from me, you beast!' she yelled.

The animal crept closer, his eyes glittering and his tongue dripping with drool. Kerry stepped backwards but stumbled over a loose stone and tripped. She fell back onto the rocks. Aware that the jackal was ready to pounce, she picked up a fist full of gravel and flung it at him. He howled and then lunged at her.

Kerry screamed.

Suddenly, with a mighty cry Grinwick appeared from over the incline with his huge claws outstretched. He descended and caught the wild dog up in a vice-like grip. Then he lifted him up high in the air. The dangling creature howled for mercy. Grinwick flew out over a precipice and dropped the jackal. With a shrill cry it landed on a ledge below and scurried away to safety. Quickly, Grinwick returned to where Kerry stood ready to swoop on another pack member. But they had already fled down the mountain after their leader.

❂❂❂

That night Farradore returned to Coracle to tell Browdan the latest news gathered by his scouts. He informed him that the Abbey had once again been deserted by Red Beak.

'The birds on watch there noticed that it was suspiciously quiet throughout the afternoon', said Farradore, 'so I led a flock of volunteers into the Abbey with me to check it out. We forced back the eagles that guarded the Abbey door and when we entered it we found that almost all eagles had vacated the building. Only a few remained to hold the fort.'

'Did they tell you where Red Beak had gone?'

'No. We got no information out of them. So we made a thorough search of the Abbey and found no clues as to where they had flown. Then I sent some scouts to check Cooley House, thinking that Red Beak had moved his camp back there. But the Eagle King and his army weren't there either. And the scouts couldn't find any trace of them.'

Browdan looked worried.

'I'm sure the eagles are devising some clever scheme of destruction for us. Have you any clue where they have vanished to?'

'They have abandoned all their usual haunts. It's a mystery.'

'Then they must have gone underground somewhere beneath the Abbey. I don't think they'll make it far through the subterranean network. Eagles only go into the caves when they're desperate. I expect they'll emerge with a surprise attack sooner or later. We must keep working on building up the town's defences and be ready to attack them when they surface.'

✿✿✿

Grinwick and the swiftails led Kerry and Niamh to the mouth of a great cave that opened as an archway into the mountain. The entrance was guarded by a flock of eagle hens in red plumes who had already been informed that they were arriving. They stood back to allow the visitors to pass through. Grinwick led them into a vaulted arcade, lit at intervals by lanterns on the floor. A series of high arched caves ran deep into the mountain and the visitors continued until they reached the entrance to an inner cavern. It had a deep red curtain draped across it.

Two tall eagle hens stood guarding the mouth of the cavern. They were also dressed in bright red plumes. One of them asked Grinwick for their names. Then she entered the inner chamber to announce the visitor's arrival.

A flock of eagle guards emerged from behind the curtain to escort Niamh, Kerry, Grinwick and the swiftails inside.

Kerry gasped when she saw the sparkling crystal chamber that glittered before her. Like a thousand chandeliers, the crystals shimmered in candlelight. The cave floor was studded with pyramids of gleaming amethysts and lit with flickering candles.

Queen Kiki rose from her perch in the centre of the chamber where she was surrounded by a nest of adoring hens. Wearing a gown of violet and white feathers her wings were studded with amethysts. The glittering, downy vision glided over to meet her visitors.

'We've been expecting you,' she said. 'Grinwick and your swiftail friends told me that you were coming to talk with me. I am very eager to hear what you're doing here and what you've got to say for yourselves.'

'Queen Kiki,' said Kerry, 'we need your help.'

'My help!' cried the Queen. 'What could I possibly do for you?'

'Is our friend Pod here?'

'The Blue Owl!' said the Queen. 'So that's what this is about. The owl is my property. My husband bought him for me at great expense. We treated him very well and gave him the best of everything. What nerve you have coming to my home on Eyrie Island to steal him from us.'

'Red Beak doesn't own him. He abducted him on the Ark of Dun Ruah when we were travelling from our home in the town of Kilbeggin. Pod is a free bird. He was never for sale. Can't you see Red Beak has lied to you about everything? He murdered the leader of this island and his wife and threw the people off their land and their homes.'

'I don't have to listen to any more of this nonsense. Is that all you came here to say?'

'Your Majesty, I have put myself and my friends in great danger by coming here to talk to you. We are at your mercy. I wouldn't have come here if I didn't think you were a good queen. Surely you know what your husband is like.'

'I do know what he is like. But you tricked me, Kerry, and made me look like a fool in front of my whole court with that laughing gas stunt. How can I trust you after that? This could be another one of your tricks.'

'Search me, Queen Kiki. I'm not here to trick you. You know I'm telling you the truth.'

Then Kerry turned to Niamh, took her by the hand and led her towards the Queen.

'This is Niamh, the daughter of the old chief of the island, Coleman Cooley. She will tell you what destruction and murder Red Beak has carried out here. And look, here is

Grinwick, a native Giant Eagle. Ask him about what Red Beak has done to terrorise the flocks of the island and bring them under his control.'

Kiki looked at Niamh and Grinwick and then sighed. She turned her back to them and fluttered slowly back to her perch.

'The Blue Owl isn't here,' she said after a long pause. 'I went back to the Abbey to get him but Red Beak had already moved him somewhere else. I don't know where he is. So I'm afraid I can't help you. You came all this way for nothing.'

Kerry looked at Niamh in desperation.

Niamh walked over to Queen Kiki's perch.

'You can help us by joining the White Army,' she pleaded. 'You said you looked foolish after Kerry's laughing gas incident. But remember what Red Beak did to her. He kidnapped her friend Pod and when she came here to search for him he imprisoned her in the dungeons. He then sent a guard to pluck Pod's feathers. Think of how painful that would have been.'

'But Red Beak told me that plucking the owl would be painless. He said he would inject him with a sedative. The owl was happy to do it until you came along.'

'Pod wasn't happy,' said Kerry. 'Red Beak forcefully injected him with a feather-growing formula. And now he can't even fly. He is weighed down with those feathers and the last time I saw him he could barely breathe. Then he risked his life for us in the forest as we tried to escape.'

'And I have seen Red Beak inflict torture on countless eagles,' added Grinwick. 'He even built a prison tower complete with torture chambers especially for this work. You must have heard the screams, Queen Kiki.'

'Well, he explained that to me by saying that his prisoners were fighting among themselves in the tower. Yes, I've always worried about Red Beak. And I know my husband is a liar. But I still love him. Is that so wrong?'

'No, it's not wrong to love someone,' said Kerry. 'Red Beak is very lucky to have someone like you to love him. And if he loves you he will listen to you. So come and help us find Pod and free the islanders. Help us persuade Red Beak to give them back their inheritance before he destroys it.'

CHAPTER 25

The Storm

The next morning a huge squall came from the sea. Farradore's forecasts for the weather proved to be correct. Dark clouds hung over the island. It was clear that a storm was brewing. As the day wore on, the weather worsened and the rain began to pour heavily. The villagers were forced indoors as the rains flooded the streets.

Browdan was busy hatching out a new defence plan in the town hall with his team of leaders. Simon was given a large division of men and women to work on new weapons. As well as building up their supply of grenades and missiles, they created mortars to launch their artillery. The leaders liaised with the villagers on strengthening the town's defences.

At noon Grinwick flew through the main door of the town hall followed by the swiftails and a flock of eagles. Everyone dropped their work and gathered to hear what they had to say.

'The chapel at the cliff top at the edge of the village is full of Red Beak's battalions,' announced Grinwick. 'There are hundreds of eagles in there, maybe thousands. Queen Kiki sent us to tell you the news.'

'But how did Red Beak's forces get into the chapel without anyone seeing them?' asked Cian. 'Our scouts have been patrolling this whole region night and day.'

'They must have used an underground passage,' declared Browdan. 'They've found the Pilgrim's Way! That's why Farradore couldn't find them in the Abbey. Red Beak has managed to get into the ancient underground path from the Abbey to the chapel on the cliff. They followed the footsteps of Niamh and Coleman. I never expected this. I thought those passages were too narrow for eagles to pass through.'

'You can never underestimate Red Beak's powers,' said Grinwick.

'But you made it to the Lone Peak Mountains and spoke with Queen Kiki?' said Browdan.

'Yes, Kerry and Niamh are still with her. Red Beak sent a flock of his guards to visit the Queen this morning. They told her that he was in the chapel and that he was asking her to join forces with him there.'

'And what does Queen Kiki plan to do now?'

'Queen Kiki wants to help us. She has sent some of her hens to plead with Red Beak to call off his attack on the town and to meet with her. But she thinks she can only stall him for a short while.'

'We've got to stop Red Beak's army getting out of the chapel,' said Cian. 'If we don't prevent them getting out they'll wreak havoc in the town.'

'Grinwick,' said Browdan, 'I need you to gather your scouts together and send them out to warn each household straight away. Tell everyone to barricade their homes and to get ready to defend themselves. No one is to go outside until I give further orders.'

Grinwick sent the freebirds off to spread the news around the town. They distributed smoke missiles with instructions on how to use them to every home.

'Board up your houses,' they cried, 'and light your fires. Red Beak is about to attack the town.'

The villagers barricaded their windows and doors and lit fires in their grates. They launched smoke missiles high into the air and they exploded into thick clouds of noxious black smoke. Simon hoped the smoke would keep the eagles off their rooftops and away from the streets. Huddled indoors, the townsfolk listened and waited. An eerie emptiness pervaded the deserted streets, which a few hours previously had been full of activity. The only sound to be heard was the wind blowing and the rain lashing against the rooftops.

❂❂❂

With blood-curdling battle cries, eagle flocks burst from the chapel on the cliff and descended into the streets. They used rocks and metal bars to attack the roofs, doors and windows. They landed on walls and rooftops, digging into tiles and mortar with their beaks and talons, trying to break through. People used everything they could find to block them out. But even the thick black smoke didn't keep them at bay.

'Eagle Power, Eagle Power,' they shrieked, instilling fear into the hearts of the villagers.

Simon and his team of pyrotechnicians remained at their base in the town hall with Browdan and Cian building up their stores of ammunition. Soon they were joined by Grinwick, Farradore and the Tawny Owl who had been forced off the streets by the savage eagle raids.

'The smoke missiles aren't working,' said Grinwick.

'We've got to get out on the streets and attack the eagles before they destroy the town,' said Simon.

'Let's target the chapel,' said Browdan. 'We must try and force our way in there. The only way we can beat Red Beak is to get into his camp and stop these raids on the town!'

'But the chapel is impregnable,' said Grinwick. 'They've carried metal bars with them, all the way from the dungeons in the Abbey. And they've used them to block the windows and doors. There's no way anyone can get in there.'

'There's got to be a weak point,' replied Browdan. 'How are they getting in and out?'

'Through the bell tower,' said Grinwick. 'They're using the windows under the roof of the tower to launch their raids.'

'We could burn them out,' said Browdan.

'No,' said Simon, 'in this rain it would be too difficult to set the church on fire.'

'Then the only way to hit Red Beak is to blow the entire chapel up,' said Browdan. 'We'll bombard them.'

'But what about Pod?' said Simon. 'Is he still with Queen Kiki?'

'No,' replied Grinwick. 'She told us that Red Beak has him.'

'Then he must be in the chapel,' said Simon. 'We can't blow it up without killing them all and Pod as well. But we can attack it and lay siege to it. We could try using more smoke bombs to flush them out.'

'Then we'll target the windows in the bell tower,' said Browdan.

'My team has a large batch of smoke and fire missiles ready,' said Simon. 'I'll select a suitable range of arms to fire at the windows in the tower. We'll also bring mortars to launch the missiles. I'll go now and get what we have prepared. Then we'll follow you to the chapel.'

✪✪✪

Browdan waited for the eagles to finish their latest raid on the village. He gathered a large squadron of volunteers together. As chief of the White Army he led his troops to the little chapel, which was situated high above the town. It stood balanced at the edge of the cliff, battered by the howling wind and rain. The troops quickly surrounded the church and lay siege on Red Beak.

Armed with Simon's hand missiles they launched their attack on the chapel windows. Red Beak's troops quickly reacted by blocking up the gaps in the windows with wood and metal from inside. They also reinforced the doors.

The White Army continued to batter the chapel at short range while they waited for Simon's division to arrive with the mortars. The eagles retaliated by dropping rocks and stones from the top of the bell tower, showering them with missiles from above. Browdan's men used their helmets and shields to protect themselves. They held their ground until Simon's squad arrived with six mortars. Then they prepared to attack.

'Hurry,' called Browdan, 'we'll be battered to death if we don't penetrate the bell tower fast. Launch your missiles directly at the top of the tower, Simon. And give it everything you've got.'

The six mortars were trained on the top of the bell tower. Simon ordered his squad to fire. They battered it with the first round of missiles but the tower held strong and the eagles cheered with their victory cries.

'Eagle Power, Eagle Power,' they chanted.

'Fire again,' Browdan cried.

Simon's team loaded the mortars and fired again. Slates fell from the roof of the tower and cracks appeared high up on the walls but still the structure held strong.

Once again Simon launched his missiles at the top of the tower. This time more of the roof tiles slid off and several eagles were hit. They fell screaming from the tower.

'You can do it, Simon,' cried Browdan. 'Give it another round.'

'Fire!' cried Simon.

Roof tiles flew and a huge gaping hole appeared in the roof but the tower stayed standing. The cries of eagles could be heard from inside as the dust and rubble flew.

'Only one round left,' cried Simon. 'It's our last shot. Here we go.'

The mortars were loaded with the last round of missiles.

'Fire,' Simon roared. The missiles flew.

With a mighty crack the entire roof of the bell tower blew off, rocking the building to its foundations. A rumbling began as the tower crumbled to the ground in a cloud of dust and rubble. Soon a gaping hole appeared where the tower joined the chapel.

Hundreds of eagles flew out of the falling tower of rubble trying desperately to enter the chapel through the gaping hole.

Browdan called on his forces to attack the base of the collapsed tower.

'Force your way through into the chapel,' he ordered.

Clouds of dust and flocks of panicking eagles blocked their path into the chapel. Each time they tried to break through, a wall of eagle wings rose up to meet them, barring their way. The force of hundreds of flapping wings created a mighty wind. The White Army were blown backwards by its surprising force.

'Use more ammunition,' ordered Browdan.

'We're out of missiles,' called Simon. 'All we have left is a batch of smoke bombs. If we can direct them into the church, the fumes might flush the eagles out.'

'Let's give it a try!'

When Browdan's men retreated from the ruins of the tower, scores of eagles emerged from inside. Armed with rubble they started to block up the gap in the wall. Simon launched a round of smoke bombs with the mortars. The bombs flew towards their target. But they were blocked down by squads of eagles who flung their bodies at the gap in the wall. For every eagle that fell another one flew in to replace him. Behind the front line more eagle reinforcements arrived to rebuild the chapel walls using the rubble from the ruins of the tower.

The White Army held their camp outside the chapel, firing round after round of smoke bombs. But the impact wasn't strong enough to penetrate the wall of eagles. And the smoke blew back into their own faces. Browdan sent to the town hall for the salvaged ammunition from the shipwrecks. It was clear that the White Army's attack on the chapel wasn't going to be easy.

The White Army kept up the siege on the chapel throughout the night. They bombarded it with further rounds of grenades. But Red Beak used organised lines of gliding eagles to repair the damaged walls. After every new attack a fresh line of eagles rose to repair the previous breaches. Simon and Browdan persisted, using every missile they could make. And Red Beak used a constant stream of his loyal subjects to repair the damage. Daylight came and still his forces defended the chapel without tiring or faltering.

Exhausted and out of ammunition, Browdan finally ordered the White Army to retreat to the town hall. Undefeated, Red Beak and his eagles remained sealed inside the chapel.

CHAPTER 26

Return of the Ark

In the morning, spirits were low in the town of Coracle. The rain continued to fall in torrents. Even Simon couldn't think of a way to defeat Red Beak. His team of technicians were already working to create new batches of ammunition. But he knew that it would be hard to beat Red Beak's ingenuity and to defeat his loyal troops. Once again small flocks of eagle scouts were flying high over Coracle, scanning the streets for weak points to attack.

'Where is the famous Messenger now that we need him?' complained Simon.

'I know Malachy won't let us down,' said Cian.

'He'll be here when we need him most,' said Dot. 'I'm going to the seafront to look out for him.'

Dot flew out and perched on the sea wall before a gale-force wind. The waves rose higher and the skies grew darker than before. The storm raged and the heavens burst open, sending down such a flood that Red Beak's roaming scouts had to flee back to the chapel.

The storm raged all day, keeping Red Beak's hordes confined indoors. The Tawny Owl brought news that Kiki and her army were camping in Cooley House ready to support the White Army when the rains died down.

'Niamh has found an underground passage in Cooley House that leads back to the town hall,' he said. 'She and Kerry are on their way back here.'

'What underground passage?' Browdan demanded.

'The only passage I know of that runs from Cooley House to Coracle joins up with the Pilgrim's Way. They could be heading straight for Red Beak's base in the old chapel.'

'We've got to stop them!' cried Simon.

'I'll go back to Cooley House,' said Grinwick. 'The wind is blowing that way and with any luck I'll get there in time to stop them.'

Grinwick immediately left them and flew towards Cooley House accompanied by a small flock of freebirds.

'I don't think he'll make it,' said Browdan looking out at the storm. 'Malachy is our only hope.'

'But now is the time we need him the most,' said Simon. 'And where is he? I know you all think the man is some kind of great hero. But he's been missing for all our battles. If he really was a prophet wouldn't he know how badly we need him now?'

'Malachy's ways are mysterious. But he won't let us down. That much I'm sure of,' said Browdan.

'Look out,' shouted Cian. 'Red Beak's eagles are roaming the streets again. They seem to be congregating on the roof above us.'

It was clear from the numbers of eagles assembling on the town hall roof that Red Beak was focusing his next attack on the White Army's base. Within minutes the eagle army launched a full-force blitz on the building. They hacked at the walls by pecking at its weak points. Simon opened some windows and fired rounds of missiles in defence but the eagles flew straight into the mortars, sacrificing their lives for their King. Soon the mortars were jammed. Simon was forced to baton down the windows and retreat inside to repair the damage. The old brickwork on the town hall walls started to crumble as flocks of eagle soldiers started penetrating the top floor.

Legion after legion of eagle forces flung themselves upon the town hall. Browdan's key volunteers were trapped inside. They barricaded the doors and windows with every stick of furniture they could find but the eagles zoned in on the roof and started taking it apart. Bit by bit the roof tiles were uplifted and flung to the ground. Soon the damage was irreparable and the eagles forced their way into the building. They swept through corridors and rooms shattering everything in their path. Browdan and his volunteers raced to the ground floor and tried to escape through a side door. But the eagles had the building fully surrounded.

Trapped in an alley and armed with hand grenades, the volunteers made their last stand against the enemy. Eagles poured into the alley from all sides. There was no escape. Hundreds of troops pounced on the White Army leaders, seized them and hauled them up into the sky.

Simon and Browdan and Cian were carried in the eagles' clutches, through the stormy gales, through the streets of Coracle and up to the chapel on the cliff. It stood precariously balanced at the edge of the seafront. The waves lashed against the sea wall as if they were trying to devour it, but the chapel still clung to its foundations. As the rebels approached, a flock of eagles flew out to meet them and escorted them through the main doors of the chapel.

Red Beak stood on the pulpit looking down on his huge audience of loyal supporters. Simon could see Pod tied up and shivering in a cage beside Red Beak. The White Army leaders were marched up the centre aisle with hundreds of eagle eyes fixed on their every move from the pews, the balconies and the rafters of the old church. The winds continued to rage outside and lightning flashed across the tall gothic windows.

Red Beak roared, his scream echoing throughout the vaults of the high ceiling. 'Search them!'

Simon was dragged before the Eagle King and stripped of his matches and weapons. Browdan and Cian's armour and weapons were confiscated.

❂❂❂

Outside Dot and Timmy waited at the shore for some sign of Malachy. Dot spotted something on the horizon and waved towards it.

'It's a ship,' she cried trying to shout over the noise of the wailing wind and water.

Within moments the Ark of Dun Ruah came into view, travelling at great speed towards the shore. Many of the villagers ran out of their homes, battling against the driving rain to see the great ship return to Coracle.

'Why isn't she dropping her anchor?' the people cried. 'She'll wreck herself against the sea wall.'

The ship continued to surge towards them, carried in full flight by the gale force winds.

'Is there no one on board?' cried Dot.

'Look, there is someone standing at the mast,' said Timmy. 'It's Malachy. He must be out of his mind.'

Malachy stood at the centre of the ship's deck. His whole body was gleaming with streaming rain, which had drenched him through to the skin. His arms were raised high over his head reaching up to the heavens. The ship was heading on a certain voyage of doom, straight towards the cliff. The onlookers held their breaths waiting for the final impact.

Suddenly, the heavens burst open and a huge flash of forked lightning struck down into Malachy's two arms. The Messenger's body lit up like the sun sending rays of flashing light out through his arms into the dark sky, turning night into day. The Ark of Dun Ruah ploughed forward on her course of destruction.

❁❁❁

'You thought you could bring me to my knees', Red Beak raged as he stood before his prisoners, 'but you underestimated my strength. I have outwitted you and counteracted every one of your onslaughts. And now look at you here grovelling at my feet.'

'We are not grovelling. This isn't over yet,' said Browdan. 'You have only captured three of us. But the White Army and its allies won't let us down.'

'Allies,' laughed Red Beak. 'Do you mean those two girls we found in the tunnel? Bring them before me, guards.'

The guards dragged Niamh and Kerry into the chapel and flung them on the floor.

'So these are your allies,' laughed Red Beak. 'They're not much use to you now!'

'Leave them alone,' yelled Simon.

'I have no pity for them,' continued the Eagle King. 'I have no pity for any of you. You thought that you could take what is rightly mine away from me. Well, you have lost the war, Browdan. You and your friends will suffer terrible deaths. I will tear every hair from your heads and every limb from your bodies. You will suffer such torture that you will cry on your bended knees for mercy.'

'Let the girls go,' cried Browdan. 'What harm have they done?'

'Scheming busybodies!' screamed Red Beak. 'Kerry Macken thought she could outsmart me and take the Blue Owl from my Queen Kiki. If it weren't for her, Kiki would have her royal cloak of blue feathers by now. She would be here by my side where she belongs. I'll have no mercy on that girl or on any of you. Guards, seize them,' he roared, 'and throw them at my feet.'

The prisoners were dragged to the foot of the pulpit. Red Beak's guards tied them to pillars. Simon struggled to find some way to defend his friends but the strongest guards overpowered him and threw him to the ground. Ten powerful eagles stood before them. Kerry saw that they had extremely long, sharp talons.

'Use your claws,' screeched Red Beak, 'and make them suffer.'

Kerry remembered Malachy's last words to her before he left the island. She knew that the moment to call him had arrived. He had made a promise to be there when she called his name.

'Malachy,' she cried. 'Malachy, where are you. We need you!'

Lightning tore through the windows, shattering the glass and breaking the metal bars into fragments. The sea wall tore open as the enormous Ark of Dun Ruah ripped straight through the church, tearing it apart. The ship front plunged towards Red Beak, who was standing high up on his pulpit. It hit him between his two red eyes and knocked him to the floor. A blood-curdling howl pierced their ears. A deep reverberating tremor shook the foundations of the chapel. The sea wall crumbled in a cloud of debris and collapsed into the violent waters below. In a frenzy of terror, the eagles flew through the gap and vanished into the night sky.

CHAPTER 27

The Sword of Truth

Malachy stood at the mast of the Ark of Dun Ruah as the great ship crashed through the walls of the old chapel. Pod's cage flew off the pulpit and hurtled towards the floor. Pillars and walls collapsed and crumbled into mounds of broken wood and stone. Shards of shattered glass splintered as they whizzed through the air. Inside the chapel a thick mist of dust and debris rose and billowed into a cloud. It covered the floor in a thick white layer. The eagles' cries rose into the heavens as they fled in terror.

Malachy jumped from the ship's bow.

He ran towards Kerry, Niamh, Simon and Browdan and quickly freed them from their tethers.

Then he started searching for Pod's cage. It lay buried somewhere beneath the rubble strewn over the chapel floor. A thick veil of dust was settling over the pews. Malachy was already wading through the debris, pulling up toppled statues and pillars. The others joined in the search but it was Malachy who found the ruined cage.

They all ran to his side as he dug the mangled shards of Pod's cage out from under some fallen beams. Pod was lying unconscious at the bottom of his metal prison, his feathers all covered in grey dust.

'Stop, the owl is mine!' screamed a voice from above them.

They looked up at Red Beak.

He stood high up on the remaining rafters of the chapel with his mighty wings outstretched. His red eyes gleamed with hatred.

'Get out of here,' Malachy ordered the friends. 'I'll deal with Red Beak. Quick, run!'

'I'm not leaving without Pod,' cried Simon.

He lunged at the cage, grabbed it from Malachy and made to escape.

With a shrill scream Red Beak flew from the rafters and descended on Simon with his claws outstretched. He plunged his sharp talons into Simon's shoulders, piercing him till blood ran down his chest. In his agony Simon dropped the cage and Red Beak grabbed it. He flew up high into the rafters carrying the cage with him.

'You'll never get the owl,' Red Beak snarled, 'and this island will always be mine. You'll never break my power.'

A blinding bolt of lightning flashed across the chapel.

Malachy stood with his arms outstretched. The lightning coursed through his body illuminating him like a dazzling star in the darkness. Light emanated from his presence with a shining radiance. He raised his arms high and stretched them towards the Eagle King. Bolts of lightning radiated from his limbs and shot up into the rafters. Electric charges vibrated across the floor. The rafters burst into flames and Red Beak flew screaming into the air.

Pod's cage tumbled towards the ground.

In a flash Malachy was beneath it. He caught the falling cage in his arms.

'Simon,' he called, 'take the owl, and this time hold on to him!'

'Never,' Red Beak's voice called from above them.

The Giant Eagle King flew at Simon with talons outstretched. But Malachy got there before him. 'You'll have to take me first,' he challenged Red Beak.

Red Beak hovered. 'If you think you have the power to defeat the great Red Beak, King of the Eagles then you are more foolish than I thought.'

'What power do you have, Red Beak?' cried the prophet. 'Show me. I'm waiting.'

Red Beak flew at Malachy but he raised his cloak as a shield. It swirled up in a rushing wind and flung the huge eagle across the chapel floor.

Red Beak rose again from the floor, his mighty wings outstretched and his claws ready to pounce. Malachy stepped towards him and appeared to rise to twice his former height. His green eyes flashed as he pulled a silver sword from a sheath hidden in his clothing. He raised the sword in the air.

Red Beak laughed. 'Never has a man's sword drawn blood

from the great Red Beak,' he cried, lunging at Malachy.

'This is the Double-Edged Sword of Truth and its power can separate bone from marrow,' cried Malachy as he aimed it at the eagle.

With a mighty flash, the ancient sword shot through the chapel and pierced the eagle in mid-flight, wounding him in the underbelly. Red Beak fell to the ground as he let out a great cry of anguish. The rafters shook and with a roar of thunder the roof caved in all around him. Lightning ripped across the floor. His body lay shattered in the smouldering silence.

Red Beak was at last defeated and broken.

❈❈❈

Malachy rushed to Simon's side. The boy lifted Pod gently from the cage and held him tenderly in his arms. Kerry, Niamh, Cian and Browdan appeared out of the ruins where they had watched the great battle and Red Beak's fall.

'Pod's got a broken wing,' said Simon, 'and he's bleeding. But he's still alive. I can feel a faint pulse.'

'Take him back to the town hall,' said Malachy. 'The chapel is dangerous. These walls are ready to crash into the sea at any minute. Hurry now before it's too late.'

'Malachy, please come with us?' pleaded Kerry.

'Not now. I will follow you, Kerry. Quickly, hurry before more of you get injured.'

Outside the chapel doors the villagers arrived accompanied by Queen Kiki and her flocks. The villagers followed Pod and his friends back to the town hall. A silent Queen Kiki entered the ruined chapel to search for her husband.

Pod was still unconscious when they arrived in the town hall. The building was in ruins but the villagers worked together to clear up the destruction caused by Red Beak's army and make some rooms comfortable for the night. Despite their weariness, the little group was unable to rest. They were worried about Pod's condition. Simon stayed up all night nursing Pod in his arms. Kerry and Niamh helped him to bathe the owl's feathers and clean the injured wing. Timmy and Dot perched by his side chirping softly, trying to breathe some life back into their old friend's battered body. By morning Pod still hadn't regained consciousness. His breathing was more laboured. Browdan called to see how he was faring and asked if there was anything he could do.

'Please go and fetch Malachy,' Kerry asked. 'There must be something he can do for Pod.'

'Malachy has been out all night helping the monks salvage their ship from the cliff face. He is also assisting the villagers in reclaiming their homes. Maybe we should leave him alone. He knows where Pod is. If he thought he could help, I know he'd be here.'

'But look at Pod,' said Kerry. 'I'm so worried about him. I'm afraid he's going to die.'

'Pod is an old bird,' said Dot. 'He's always been nervous and excitable. He has had a weak heart for years. His pulse is very faint. The owl has been through an awful lot. I think Red Beak injected him with more feather-growing formula since we last saw him. His body is very bloated and even thicker with feathers. The extra weight and strain might have been too much for Pod's heart. We'll be lucky if he pulls through.'

'But Malachy can save him,' cried Kerry.

'You don't know that,' said Niamh. 'If there was anything he could do, I'm sure he'd be here.'

'Maybe he doesn't know how weak Pod is,' said Kerry.

'Alright Kerry,' said Browdan, 'I'll go to him on your behalf and tell him that you are asking for him.' Then he left them.

❁❁❁

Later in the morning Malachy called to the town hall to enquire about Pod.

'Oh, I knew you'd come,' said Kerry rushing to meet him. 'I knew you wouldn't desert Pod.'

'Kerry, you must understand there are things I can't interfere in. Pod needs you to be there for him. And the islanders need me. They have a great burden of work to do. They need my help even more than Pod does. Trust me.'

Kerry hung her head.

'Where is Browdan?' said Malachy. 'I've got something to give him.'

Browdan was already standing at Malachy's side.

'While we were moving the Ark of Dun Ruah from the ruins of the old chapel', said Malachy, 'I found something that I know you will treasure.'

He held out his closed fist and opened it. Browdan gasped to see his father's sapphire ring glittering in its radiant blue glory. It was the chieftain's ring that had been handed down through generations to his father. Coleman Cooley had always worn it until Red Beak had prised it from him at his death.

'I found it on the chapel floor under the pulpit. I saw it fall from Red Beak's talon just before he fell.'

The dazzling deep blue stone lay sparkling in Malachy's hand.

'Take it and treasure it,' Malachy said, giving the ring to Browdan.

'Think of your father while you wear it. This stone has passed from chieftain to chieftain of this island from ancient times. It is your inheritance. And it is a symbol of a greater treasure, that of true wisdom. You have been blessed to inherit your father's wisdom and knowledge. This ring is a symbol of the treasures within you. Guard them and nurture their goodness. You will make a great chieftain, Browdan.'

Browdan took the ring from Malachy's hands and just as he slipped it onto his finger Pod stirred in Simon's arms. They all gathered around him.

Pod opened his amber eyes and rested them on his little group of friends. 'So you all went off and left me alone in the woods with Red Beak's terrible army,' he said. 'What kind of friends are you?'

'I'm so sorry, Pod,' cried Kerry. 'It's my fault. I shouldn't have let you out of my sight. And I should never have brought you on this trip in the first place.'

Pod's bright eyes smiled at Kerry.

'Then I wouldn't have gotten the chance to be a hero. It wasn't your fault, Kerry. I'm just a tired old owl. My wings aren't what they used to be. They just gave up. But don't worry about me. It's time for me to go to the Ocean's End and rest.'

'But, Pod, you can't leave us now,' cried Kerry. 'And why are you talking about Ocean's End?'

'Ocean's End is a great place for old owls. There are miles of open skies for me to glide through and peaceful forests where I can regain my strength. I'm hoping to get a fresh pair of wings. Don't worry about me. I've got lots of friends waiting for me there.'

'Then we'll come with you,' said Kerry.

'No. This is something I've got to do on my own. It's time for me to leave you at last. But I'm glad I got to spend so much time with someone as beautiful as you. I'll always be your friend, Kerry, remember that. Keep me in your heart.'

Then Pod looked at Simon.

'Take me to the old chapel on the cliff Simon. That's a good place for me to fly to Ocean's End. It's time for me to go. We must hurry while I still have some strength.'

Simon lifted Pod onto his shoulder and although the owl's coat was thick with layers of rich, blue feathers, his body felt light. Simon carried him through the streets of Coracle followed by his group of friends and many of the villagers. Soon they reached the ruins of the old chapel which had been ripped apart by the Ark of Dun Ruah. Already the ship had been hauled over to Coracle harbour by the monks and villagers. From the clifftop they could see them busily working on her restoration. There they all stood, clustered around Pod at the edge of the cliff, facing out over the sea.

Browdan came forward and stood before Simon and Pod. 'We will always remember you for what you did, Pod. Your courage and bravery have been a huge blessing to everyone on this island. If it wasn't for you we would be still living in the caves and hiding from the evil Red Beak. Thanks to the sacrifice you made for your friends, we have our beautiful island back. We'll never forget you, dear friend.'

'I don't deserve this honour,' said Pod. 'In the short time I've been here I've grown to love this island. It was a small price to pay. Now I must go before my wings entirely fail me. Goodbye to all my friends.'

Then he looked at Simon. 'Take care of your sister and of those two little swiftails. And be careful with the matches. How many times have I told you they're dangerous?'

'Oh, Pod, don't leave us,' cried Kerry. 'Please, please stay. I can't bear to say goodbye.'

Niamh placed a hand on Kerry's shoulder. 'Let him go, Kerry,' she said.

Kerry reached out to stroke Pod's breast. Then she looked into his amber eyes. 'Goodbye, my brave friend,' she said. 'I'll miss you so very much.'

Pod's head had tilted to one side. His glittering eyes filled with golden warmth. Kerry saw a little flutter inside his breast and then he lifted his wings to fly. He glided out over the clifftop and hovered there for a moment looking back at his friends. Then he drifted out over the waves and flew into the distant blue horizon.

Instead of feeling sad, Kerry suddenly felt lighter. It was as if a heavy cloud had been lifted from her heart. The air grew sweet and crystal clearness descended over the clifftop. She could hear the sound of Pod's hooting ringing across the heavens.

The little group stood gazing out over the Sea of Sorrows until the sun set. As they walked back to the town of Coracle, Kerry looked down over its calm blue harbour and at the people working there to bring the island back to life. The curse of Red Beak was broken, the water spirits were silent and the sea was at peace.

CHAPTER 28

New Beginnings

That night Malachy came to visit Kerry in the town hall. The villagers had worked hard during the day to repair the roof and make it comfortable for the night. Victory was sweet and peace reigned on the island but Kerry felt a deep sorrow in her heart for the loss of her friend Pod. She sat with Malachy high up on the town hall terrace overlooking the town of Coracle and the silent sea beyond.

Malachy told Kerry that the monks had made good progress on the restoration of the Ark of Dun Ruah. The ship would be restored within a few days and ready to take her to the Land of Fire with Simon and the swiftails. Despite the great blow it had received hitting the chapel wall, the repairs it needed were quite minor. The Abbot had kindly offered to place a crew of his best seafaring monks at their disposal.

'But I don't want to leave the island without Pod,' said Kerry.

'Pod has gone on an exciting new adventure of his own,

Kerry. And now it's time for you to get on with your life.'

'You don't understand.'

'Maybe I do understand something,' said Malachy. 'Would I be right in saying that you blame me for what happened to Pod?'

'Why couldn't you help him Malachy? I believe you could have healed him if you put your mind to it. But you didn't want to. You just let him go. What's the point in having all these miraculous powers if you don't use them?'

'I'm really a very simple man, Kerry. I'm a great lover of nature and I've learnt the discipline of keeping my eyes and ears open. I've studied the weather and the seas and the skies. I have trained myself to listen carefully to what the people and creatures of this planet tell me. I just watch. I know that Pod was happy to sacrifice himself for you and the islanders. It was his choice to give his life to save you. He choose to be a hero. And I know he is going to a good place now. It's a place where he can rest and be restored!'

'But why did he have to leave us?' Kerry asked.

'It was his choice Kerry.'

'But I miss his voice.'

'Keep his memory in your heart. You are a lucky girl to have a great future ahead of you. You have been blessed by the one who is much greater than all of us. Develop your gifts and use them the way God created you to use them.'

'I wish I could just stay here with you and my friends. Why can't we all stay together on this beautiful island?'

'Things always change. Adventures end and new ones begin.

Remember the words of the prophet who wrote:

Do not dwell on the past.
See I am doing a new thing!
Now it springs up; do you not perceive it?
I am making a way in the desert
and streams in the wasteland.
The wild animals honour me,
the jackals and the owls,
because I provide water in the desert.'

'That's the same scripture we found in the Abbey,' said Kerry. 'It was written on the last page of the manuscript in the library! Pod read it to me. You knew it, Malachy! You were there.'

'I was keeping an eye on you, my child. And I always will.'

'Will you come with us Malachy?'

'Your brother and your friends will be with you. The Abbot wants me to stay here to help the islanders with rebuilding their lives. And I will do that until the Great Creator of the universe calls me somewhere else. But don't worry, child. This is not the last you've seen of the Messenger. There will be many more adventures. And remember, whenever you need me, Kerry, just whisper the words to the wind and I promise I'll be there.'

'I'll miss you, Malachy. I'll miss all my friends on this island.'

Malachy looked at her thoughtfully. 'But now you must think about the future. What about that famous trip to the Land of Fire? President Lumina is waiting for you.'

❂❂❂

On a clear blue morning the Ark of Dun Ruah was ready to set sail. Kerry, Simon and the swiftails were saying goodbye to their friends at the pier in Coracle when a flock of eagles appeared on the horizon and made straight for the village. Kerry saw that Queen Kiki was at the head of the flock. She quickly descended and alighted with her entourage before Kerry on the pier wall. She wore a silver crown of jewels in many colours and a long headress of black feathers.

'I've come to say goodbye,' said Kiki. 'And I want to thank you for telling me the truth about my husband when you came to see me at the Lone Peak. I didn't want to hear it at the time, Kerry. Sometimes the truth is the last thing we want to hear.'

'You are a wise queen,' said Kerry. 'Will you stay here on the Isle of Dun Ruah and lead the colony?'

'Red Beak is still alive,' said Kiki. 'He is hanging on by a thread. I've thought about leaving him and going back to my family but I can't. I will stay loyal to him. It sounds crazy but I do love him still, Kerry. His power is broken and I will be there for him if he needs me. I hope that I can be a good influence on my husband if he recovers. And I'm sorry for all the pain he has caused you.'

Kerry reached out to embrace the Eagle Queen. 'Where will I find you when I come to visit Coracle?' she said.

'In my Crystal Chamber, of course,' laughed Queen Kiki, 'on the Lone Peak Mountains. It is beautiful there, far more comfortable than the Abbey. And much more fitting for an Eagle Queen. You know, despite all the work we did to the

Abbey, it was never suited to be a palace!'

'I'll see you at the Crystal Chamber then,' called Kerry as she boarded the Ark of Dun Ruah with Simon and the swiftails. She gazed out over the Sea of Sorrows on the beautiful island where Browdan, Niamh, Coleman, Grinwick and all the birds and villagers of Coracle stood to wave them off.

As the ship sailed across the peaceful waters, Kerry thought she heard a faint hooting call above her. She looked up at the mast and she saw two amber eyes looking down. There was a flutter of blue feathers as the bird flew high up into the heavens and disappeared.

Then she remembered the owl's last words.

'I'll always be your friend, Kerry, remember that. Keep me close to your heart.'

Protectors of the Flame

CHAPTER 1

Protectors of the Flame

Kerry sat at the window of Macken Cottage gazing out into the garden. She searched for some sign of her brother and wondered what was taking him so long. Her wide, blue eyes scanned the line of old oak trees that skirted the bottom of the garden where the Swishtree Forest began. Earlier she had seen the THING staring at her through the trees again. She was being watched, she was sure of it now. It was beginning to haunt her dreams.

'Simon's been gone for ages,' she complained, drumming her fingers on the windowsill. 'When I asked him to check the garden I didn't think it would take this long!'

'Maybe he found the THING!' said Timmy.

'That's what worries me ...'

'Look there's a light in the shed,' cried Dot, darting onto Kerry's shoulder.

They stared through the fading autumn sunlight at the

flickering bulb inside the shed window. Something was wrong in there and Kerry knew it. A low rumble echoed around them like distant thunder. Suddenly, a rapid series of bright green flashes lit up the shed.

BOOM!

A deafening explosion hit their ears. The sky lit up. And a blaze of fire burst from the shed. The kitchen window cracked open. Beneath them the floorboards rocked. Shards of glass sprayed onto the counter top, shattering all over the floor. The kitchen dresser shook violently and collapsed, sending crockery flying in all directions. Cupboard doors flew open. Saucepans rattled across the room. Plates and cups smashed into tiny pieces.

Kerry and the swiftails were flung backwards by the force of the flying glass. Kerry hit the wall and a shelf piled with jugs and tumblers crashed down onto her head. Timmy and Dot flew up to the rafters trying to escape falling debris. Broken pictures and kitchen implements fell from scattered drawers and containers. Food tins clattered across Kerry's limp body.

Then – silence.

With a loud moan, Kerry tried to free herself from the debris. She managed to push the fallen shelf off of her and raise herself to her knees. Drops of blood dripped onto the dusty rubble that covered the floor. She wondered where the blood came from. A heavy haze flooded across her brain and she swayed dangerously towards the floor. Through the fog she saw Timmy hovering before her. He fanned her face with his feathers. The soft breeze cleared the dust and the dizziness subsided.

'You OK, Kerry?' he said.

'What on earth was that?' she said as she struggled to free herself from the broken remnants of her kitchen.

'The shed's on fire,' cried Dot. 'Look out the window.'

Kerry turned to see scorching flames leaping up outside the gaping hole that had been her window.

'Simon,' Kerry yelled as she pulled herself onto her feet. She staggered to the back door and rushed towards the shed which was now completely engulfed in flames.

'Simon,' she screamed louder. She tried to get closer to the shed door. But a powerful blast of heat forced her back.

'Keep back,' came Timmy's voice close behind her. 'You'll be burned alive.'

'But Simon is in there. We've got to get him out.'

'Kerry get back from the fire,' screamed familiar voices.

She turned to see two of her neighbours running up the garden path with buckets of water in their hands. It was Tom Dillon and his son John from up the road. They ran towards the shed and emptied their buckets in through the broken window. But the fire raged on with enormous flames ripping through the roof.

'We've got to get Simon,' cried Kerry. 'He said he was going to check the shed.' She lunged towards the blaze.

'Keep back,' shouted Tom Dillon grabbing her by the arm and pulling her away from the flames. 'Do you know that there's blood pouring down your face?'

'Let me go, I've got to find Simon.'

'Get back, Kerry. You'll be burned alive if you go in there. The fire brigade are on their way. Let them do the job.'

'But he's the only family I have in the world. Let me go.'

Kerry struggled in Tom's arms but he had a tight grip. She tried to shake him off but he held her fast. She could hear the sound of sirens in the distance. People were running up the road with more buckets. Within minutes the fire brigade were on the scene smothering the blaze with their powerful hoses.

'Be careful,' yelled Kerry. 'My brother's in there.'

'We know what we're doing, young lady,' said the chief fireman. 'Now keep away from the blaze.'

Within minutes the fire brigade had the fire under control. Soon the last flames were out. Thick black smoke rose from the ruins. Kerry held her breath while the firemen entered the shed to search for Simon. They picked their way through the charred remains of his equipment. At last, when she thought she couldn't bear it any longer, the chief fireman emerged through the ruined doorway.

'There is no sign of your brother in here,' he said. 'The place is burned badly but we'd definitely see his body if he was here.'

Tears of relief sprang into Kerry's eyes. 'Are you sure?' she asked.

'Yes and you need to get some medical attention. Let Mr Dillon take you to the doctor.'

'I'm not leaving here without Simon.'

'Maybe he saw the THING,' said Dot. 'And went after it.'

'What THING?' asked the fireman.

'There was something in the garden,' said Dot. 'Simon went

out to see what it was. It was watching us through the trees.'

'What did it look like?'

'I don't know,' Kerry answered. 'Please help me! We've got to find Simon.' She wiped her hand across her forehead and gasped when she saw that it was smeared with blood.

'You've got to get that seen to, Kerry,' said Timmy. 'Look, I'll go and search the forest for Simon. He may have spotted something in there and gone after it.' Timmy flew off into the Swishtree Forest.

The chief fireman took Kerry firmly by the arm and led her towards Tom Dillon. 'My men will be here on the grounds for a while checking things out,' he said. 'Don't worry about Simon. We'll find him. Now get yourself to the doctor before you pass out.'

❂❂❂

Kerry and Dot sat in the Dillon's front sitting room waiting for news of Simon. A big wad of white gauze was wound around Kerry's head. Her face was pale. The doctor had spent the last half hour removing some fine slivers of glass from her forehead before he stitched her up. After her painful ordeal, Tom Dillon insisted on taking Kerry home to his wife for a cup of tea. Mrs Dillon did her best to make Kerry comfortable on the sofa and offered her a plate of freshly-baked brown scones. But Kerry pushed it away.

There was a loud knock on the front door.

'Stay where you are. I'll get it,' said Mrs Dillon as she hurried off to answer it.

'Oh hello, Lord Mayor,' they heard her say from the hallway. 'Yes she's here, come on in. I'll go and make you a fresh pot of tea.' She showed him into the sitting room.

'It's the Lord Mayor for you, Kerry,' she said.

Kerry rose to greet the Mayor, who swept into the room wearing a shiny blue suit.

'My dearest Kerry,' he said, 'you look absolutely awful, you poor thing. What a dreadful thing to happen. I came as soon as I could get away from the town hall.'

'Have you seen Simon?' Kerry demanded.

'No. He's still missing. But we all heard the blast of that explosion down in the town hall. It could be heard for miles and miles. Some of the old town councillors are in a state of shock. We're lucky one of them didn't drop dead. One of these days that brother of yours will blow up the entire town. Everybody is talking about it. The police are down at Macken Cottage right now asking questions. They want to talk to you about what happened before the fire.'

'Oh no!' said Kerry.

'What does that boy keep in the shed? It sounded like a nuclear explosion.'

'I'm so sorry,' said Kerry. 'Simon's been worse than ever since we came back from our trip to the Land of Fire. He's always in the shed doing some experiment or other. I'm so worried. I wish I knew where he was.'

'President Lumina told me that he's been working on a project for her.'

'Yes,' said Dot. 'He says it's top secret and that it will change the world.'

'He always says things like that,' said Kerry. 'But why haven't they found him? He's been gone so long.'

'Simon is always missing when you want him the most, Kerry,' said Dot. 'You know what he's like. Don't worry, he'll turn up soon.'

'Yes, let's look at the bright side,' said the Lord Mayor. 'They didn't find any trace of Simon in the shed, so it is possible that he's still alive. The fire brigade are still searching for him around the grounds. They said his body may have been flung from the building during the explosion. And the chief fireman has assured me that the house is fine, apart from the broken window, the ruined kitchen and smoke damage. With a few renovations it will be all back to normal. So don't worry.'

'Don't worry, you say! My brother is missing, the police want to question me, I can't afford to renovate my burned-down house and I've got a blinding headache ...'

'My dear Kerry,' said the Mayor, 'you never told me that you were having financial difficulties. President Lumina is constantly asking for you to visit her at Fire City. She's got plenty of work for you there. I can't understand why you came back.'

'I was worried about Simon falling behind with his school work. And I love being at home in Kilbeggin. It's a pity there's so little work in this town.'

'There's no point in being broke Kerry,' said the Mayor. 'I'll cover the cost of your voyage to the Land of Fire. It's the least I can do.'

'This is very kind of you but I'm not going anywhere without Simon. I'll clean the mess up myself. The fire brigade said they would board up the kitchen window until I can afford to get it replaced. I can manage … really …'

'Kerry, you simply cannot go back to that awful mess and live without windows. I wont allow you.'

At that moment there was a tapping at the window. They all leaped up and saw Timmy hovering outside. Kerry raced over to unlatch the window.

'It's OK, Kerry. I saw him,' said Timmy. 'He's in the forest.'

'Is he alive?' she cried. Large tears welled up in her eyes.

'Of course he's alive. He says someone blew the shed up.'

'I think everyone agrees that Simon blew it up,' said the Mayor.

'Why would he blow up his own shed?' asked Timmy.

'Accidents always happen when people leave dangerous chemicals lying around unattended,' said the Mayor. 'They become unstable and can explode at any time. Everybody is saying that—'

'Timmy,' shouted Kerry. 'Where is he?'

'No need to shout, Kerry,' said the Lord Mayor. 'Calm down. You're in a state of shock and it's not good for you to be getting upset. Now Timmy answer the question – Where is Simon?'

'That's what I'm trying to explain if you would only listen to me. Everybody is blaming Simon for the explosion but it wasn't his fault. You see he saw someone in the shed …'

'Who?' said the Mayor.

'He didn't tell me. He just said it wasn't safe for him to come back.'

'But that's ridiculous,' laughed the Mayor. 'Who would want to blow that old shed up?'

'Simon said that he's been working on a top secret project for President Lumina. Something called "Platinum Fire". And if it got into the wrong hands it could be very, very dangerous.'

'Dangerous!' exclaimed Kerry. 'Why would President Lumina involve him in something dangerous? Take me to him Timmy. Please, I've had enough of this.'

'I can't.'

'Why?'

'Because I don't know where he is.'